Surrogate for a Werewolf

By

Jennifer Lynne

HellBound Books

A HellBound Books
Publication
Copyright © 2017 by Jennifer Lynne
All Rights Reserved

Cover and art design by HellBound Books Publishing/Jennifer Lynne

www.hellboundbookspublishing.com

www.jenniferlynneerotica.com

Printed in the United States of America

Surrogate for a Werewolf

Prologue

The moonlight shone bright and silver through the open window, the mountain breeze that stirred the heavy curtains cool on Anichka's naked skin. Ignoring the peripheral presence of the tall, black-clad lady in the shadow-smothered far corner of the boudoir, Anichka skilfully manoeuvred herself onto all fours, shifting the heavy bulk of her pregnant belly with grace, her elbows and knees sinking into the thick, coarse fur of the bearskin rug that lay at the foot of her lover's towering, four-posted bed.

Anichka shivered with anticipation, her bare pussy pouting and moist and so incredibly impatient; her handsome lover had spent an infuriating yet delectable age lapping at her soft folds with that expert tongue of his, using its tip to massage the throbbing nub of her clitoris to near-orgasm. Of course, he'd held off at the very last moment, a trick that he knew all too well would drive his lover to distraction, that she would be even more eager than was usual to receive his formidable cock when he decided that time would come.

And that time was now.

"Are you ready for me, my love?" the resonant, baritone voice rumbled from behind her.

"Can you not see that for yourself, my lover?" Anichka replied with a lascivious laugh. She wriggled her firm, shapely rump at him, and felt her plump outer lips part and the delicate petals of her inner labia spread ever so slightly to give her lover a tantalising glimpse of her dark, wet hole.

She felt huge, powerful hands upon her hips, sensed the heat of her lover's naked body close behind, and pictured in her highly aroused mind his thick, long cock with its fierce, bulging head as it homed in on her most intimate place. Anichka braced herself for the inevitable, for the moment she had been craving since he had first placed his mouth on her aching, wet pussy and wriggled his long, lithe tongue deep inside her tight, sopping entrance. This was the part of their love making that Anichka desired the most, the moment when she was crammed so very full with her lover in his entirety, when they were joined as one in sex. And of course there was what she knew would happen once her lover was embedded deep inside the throbbing, wanton walls of her vagina – and that was the part of their love ritual that Anichka craved most of all.

Anichka pushed back onto the thick, long cock, welcoming it into the slick cleft of her vulva and arching her back ever so slightly to position it's fat, bulbous head against the entrance to her vagina; her heavy, pendulous breasts – so deliciously engorged with milk – rubbed delectably against the thick fur rug to send sensual ripples of pleasure through her stiff, leaking nipples.

She moaned out loud as her lover's penis found its mark and slipped effortlessly inside her tight, young pussy, stretching its muscles and caressing the rippled inside as it made its way deep inside her body. Powerful hands gripped Anichka's hips – almost to the point of pain – and her lover grunted with a deep, almost primeval voice as he buried his cock all the way down to its hard, broad base into her body, heavy balls bouncing freely against the swollen nub of her clit.

Slowly, masterfully, he thrust his strong hips, pounding his huge cock in and out of Anichka's body, filling her pussy up so completely, bumping hard against the rubbery nub of her cervix to send wave upon wave of sheer and absolute pleasure crashing through her naked body, grunting loudly at his own exertions.

"Change for me, my love," Anichka purred, her breath in short gasps as she pushed backwards to meet the powerful thrusts, her hand reaching between her own legs to rub frantically at her swollen clitoris, her fingers instantly slick.

Her lover let out a low, growling grunt, and Anichka felt his grip on her hips strengthen and his nails dig into the soft flesh there. She sensed the inevitable approach of orgasm, hurtling towards her like some alien, unstoppable force; this was the part of their sex ritual that never failed to make Anichka cum, and cum hard.

With the entire thickness of his cock embedded deep inside his lover's vagina, he began to transform. His body trembled and throbbed, his muscles rippled like thick liquid beneath his shifting flesh. His back arched, his chest thrust outwards and rib cage expanded as his stomach curved inwards in a graceful hollow. Coarse, black hair sprouted the length and breadth of his body, the bones in his face crunched and manoeuvred as if smashed and rearranged by mighty, unseen hands. He cried out with the sheer, abject pain of his transformation, a cry that quickly turned into the low, wailing howl of the beast he was rapidly becoming. He lifted up a freshly elongated snout, throwing his head back in the cold glow of the moonlight and he howled as the last of the metamorphosis transformed his once human body into that of a snarling, primordial beast.

Anichka cried out in unison with her lover, although *her* cries were those of pleasure, of the unimaginable orgasm that tore through her prone, vulnerable body. She clamped her fingers down hard on her hot, pulsing clit, straining against the expanding girth of her lover's cock which stuffed her vagina ever fuller, stretching it deliciously beyond capacity, cramming her with his beast-cock. And still he pumped in and out of Anichka's sopping pussy, grinding hard against her flesh, his newly transformed cock creating climax upon climax in her groaning, perspiring body, making her cry out his name, and that of her god.

Anichka felt her lover tense. It was that muscle-clenching, teeth grinding tension that she knew preceded his climax, and she knew full well the danger that presented to her with him now in his transformed state, when he was far more beast than he was man; a time at which the creature he had become could all too quickly tear her petite, exposed body apart despite the depth of his love for her.

And at that moment, Anichka was grateful for the protective presence of the woman in the shadows.

Each time they fucked, Anichka wondered if that was to be the time he would administer that longed-for bite, the breaking of her delicate flesh that would bring her fully into his way of life. Just one small bite, borne of the beast's loss of self-control that would make Anichka a beast just like her lover. But that hope had faded somewhat once she had become impregnated; in her present state, she had no idea what the consequences might be if she were to become one of the Werewolf.

Her lover yowled, and his voice carried out through the window and far off into the night. He thrust with deep, powerful strokes into Anichka's body as he exploded inside her, filling her tight, wet pussy with spurt upon spurt of hot, creamy cum that felt as if it were flowing from the root of his very soul. Anichka's muscles tightened around his cock, clenching and squeezing as she reached her final shuddering orgasm and the girl howled along with her beast lover.

Exhausted, thoroughly spent, he slumped forward, resting the powerful bulk of his body against his lover's sweat-soaked back, his arms supporting much of his weight.

Anichka buried her face into the bear skin rug, her arms collapsing into its thick pile, her rump still elevated as her lover's cock was still buried deep inside her. His fluids oozed out of her well-fucked hole and dribbled down her milky thighs in hot rivulets. Anichka sighed deeply as her body slowly descended from the dizzying heights of the pleasures that her incredible lover had delivered, as she enjoyed the feel of the rough hair of her lover's belly that equalled that of the bearskin in coarseness.

Suddenly, the door burst open. The thick, heavy wood crashed against the stone wall and there stood a tall, broad shape. It stormed into the room, sharp features illuminated by the chilling glow of the moon.

"No!?" the woman in black shouted out as she bustled out from her corner and towards the intruder.

"Leave me alone, Mistress!" the tall shape barked, swatting away the woman as if she were nothing more than a troublesome insect. The woman tumbled away, head over heels, back into her corner, the breath knocked from her lungs.

Anichka looked up from beneath her startled lover to see the woman land awkwardly - unconscious or dead – her legs splayed out before her, dress riding high and her denuded pussy twinkling wetly in the dim light.

Anichka's lover pulled away from her to confront the gatecrasher, growling deep from the pit of his belly, the hair between his shoulders stiff and bristling. He rose to his full height on his strong, beast legs and made his way across the room to where the intruder stood in a defiant stance.

Anichka couldn't help but gasp at the residual pleasure that caressed her vagina as the mighty cock slipped from her body. She lay there on the rug, too afraid to move, her eyes locked onto the heavy-set, masculine figure that stood framed by the door way, his handsome, chiselled face glowing in the moonlight.

"This has to stop," the interloper said, his voice rich and commanding. "I know that you no more want to hurt me than I do you."

Anichka's lover paid the man no heed and prowled towards him, his keen, vicious claws click-clacking against the cold stone floor. He growled again, his golden eyes narrowed to slits, teeth bared, haunches clenched and ready to pounce.

The man held his ground, refusing to be intimidated by the mighty beast his that confronted him; after so many centuries, the transformation of their species was nothing new. "She is mine," the man said, his voice calm. "We have been lovers for a long time, it is time you faced the truth."

Anichka's lover glanced over at her as she struggled to her feet on the bear skin, her hands placed protectively over her full belly, her engorged breasts resting on the swollen mound within which nestled her child.

"She loves me, and I love her," the intruder continued. "We are meant to be together." He too looked over at Anichka, with pain etched on his handsome face at seeing her pink, post-coital flush and another's seed trickling down along the inside of her thighs. "You have stolen her from me, you have always wanted what I have," he said. "Tonight, it stops."

"I love both of you," Anichka's voice was barely audible, uncharacteristically timid. "It is unfair that you should make me choose." She walked towards them, her bare feet slapping quietly on the floor, her entire body illuminated ghost-white by the sliver light that cascaded through the window, the gentle breeze raising gooseflesh across her naked breasts.

The beast stared at her in disbelief, its body beginning to make the changes back towards a more human form; hair absorbed back into skin, dripping snout receded, claws retracting.

"Tell him, Anichka," the man said, his voice echoing about the cool, stone walls. "Tell him whose child you are carrying."

Anichka stopped dead in her tracks, as if she had been physically struck. "I don't know," she whispered. "I honestly don't know."

"You told me-"

"I know I did, but the truth is that I simply do not know which of you is the father." Anichka caressed her taut, bulging belly, as if to calm the tumultuous child within her.

"The child is mine," her lover grunted, his voice strained through his beast's throat. "I know this for sure." And although his eyes remained primitive behind the hirsute and elongated shape of a werewolf, Anichka could see that his heart was breaking.

Anichka shook her head, her face sad and filled with remorse. "I fell in love with you both," she offered, "I never meant to, but I just couldn't help it."

"You *must* choose," the intruder's voice remained steady.

"I-I can't," Anichka said, tears welling in her eyes.

"Then I will choose for you," the intruder stepped towards Anichka with one vast, powerful hand outstretched. "You must come with me; you are not safe here." He looked directly at the beast who, in his half animal, half human state looked dangerously unpredictable.

"No," the beast snarled. He rounded on the man, his muzzle elongating once more and thick strings of saliva dripped from the exposed white of his canines.

The two squared up to each other, the intruder at the very least a head taller than Anichka's lover, his features beginning to shift and grow longer as his body began its own transformation. He flexed his mighty hands and scythe-like claws sprouted from each broad fingertip, razor sharp and glinting. He growled a low, warning growl, a sinister noise that resounded through the bedroom like the rumble of an oncoming earthquake.

"Stop this!" Anichka cried out, dismayed to see the two men she loved posturing and prepared to rip out each other's throats. "I love you both, can't you see that? It doesn't matter whose child this is, not to me." She moved her hands away from her naked bump, pushing it outwards to emphasise the wonderful swell of her petite frame.

"Betrayed by my own," her lover snarled, his voice almost indiscernible as once more his body adopted the primitive shape of the werewolf. He snapped his jaws mere inches away from the intruder's face and reached out his curled claws towards the intruder's heaving chest. The intruder growled and tore at the thick plaid material of his shirt, allowing his expanding chest room to grow, the entire surface of his torso smothered with thick wiry hair the color of the darkest, most decadent chocolate. He flexed his broad, muscular thighs and made ready to pounce, his lips curled upwards in a sneering snarl.

"Anichka!" the Mistress cried out as she struggled to her shaking legs in the corner of the boudoir.

Too late.

Without so much as a cry out, Anichka threw herself from the bedroom window and out into the moon soaked night. Down she fell, onto the hard and unforgiving rocks that sprawled beneath the window like so many vicious, jagged teeth.

The two werewolves dashed across the room, thick, sharp nails tapping frantically against the floor, their anger and hurt at mutual betrayal forgotten in that instant.

The sound that Anichka's small, fragile body made when it hit the rocks was one neither of them could ever forget, not even in a thousand lifetimes; a warm, wet *slap* of soft flesh against eons-hardened granite, of bones splintering with a noise akin to that of a carelessly dropped egg.

The werewolves howled out their anguish at the pale, uncaring full moon, and their cries filled the valley that stretched out beyond their imposing home to chill the souls of the people who lived in the small town on the banks of the river.

Chapter One

Alyssa Bowers sat in the luxury of the spacious doctor's office at the clinic, fiddling nervously with the hem of the skirt that in hindsight she considered to be far too short for the occasion. The tight, faded denim – fashionably frayed at the edges – had ridden up her milk-white thighs the minute she'd sat down in the plush leather chair opposite the doctor and Alyssa was convinced that he was getting more than an eyeful of her white, cotton panties.

"Of course, we can't disclose the name of the client you'd be a surrogate for," the doctor – who looked exceedingly young and handsome in his crisp, white coat and expensive shirt – told Alyssa. "We will reveal that all in good time - should you be successful. I'm sure that you understand that discretion is paramount in matters such as these."

Alyssa nodded and tried to ignore the dampness that was beginning to spread in her panties; just the thought of the dishy young doctor examining her was getting her juices flowing a treat. She ran a nervous finger around the strap of her blue halter top, all too aware that the flimsy garment showed off a goodly amount of her deliciously modest cleavage and more than a little of the unmistakable curve of sideboob. Alyssa she couldn't help but wonder if she was having a similarly arousing effect upon the doctor.

Alyssa smiled an inward smile, pleased with herself at just how far she had come in the past few months; there was a time that she would never even have *dreamed* of wearing clothes as skimpy as those she was wearing today, and certainly not for a visit to an exclusive private clinic. But this was the *All-New* Alyssa; the post-Rusty McCloud Alyssa who was finally free of the guy she'd dated since ninth grade and who'd always insisted she be demure and chaste. And who, despite Alyssa's attempts at persuasion, had cowered behind his unwavering *belief* in Jesus Christ, his Lord and saviour, and abstinence to avoid having sex with her.

Which was why, at the ripe old age of twenty-two, Alyssa Bowers remained a virgin, much to her chagrin, her friend's amusement, and despite her very best efforts at seducing her uptight boyfriend.

It was this somewhat unique situation that Alyssa found herself in that by pure happenstance had made her the perfect candidate for this particular job; something else she would never in a million lifetimes have considered back in the bad ol' Rusty days.

Of course, being two young, healthy teens growing up in a mid-sized town in the murky backwaters of rural Mississippi, Alyssa and Rusty had not abstained from *all* forms of sexual congress, which much would have been completely against the natural order of things. In fact, pretty much the only thing Rusty had *not* done with Alyssa was to fuck her pussy good and hard like she'd all too often wished for. She'd genuinely lost count of the times she'd taken Rusty's squat, meaty dick in her mouth and sucked it dry; the untold *pints* of his sticky, salty-sweet cum she must have gulped down over the years in the name of love and in order to earn her just reward of having Rusty lap at her tender, teenaged clit like a thirsty dog at a watering hole. Give the boy his due, Rusty was a demon with that tongue of his, rarely failing to hit just the right spot and make his gal cum almost to the point of screaming.

But still, what Alyssa wouldn't have given to have had her pious boyfriend's dick buried deep inside her wet, aching vagina, his balls furiously slap-slapping against the sweet, puckered hole of her ass – or even the boy's fingers venturing inside her tight entrance would have been better than the *nothing* that she did get. And all of this neglect of her vagina just left poor Alyssa feeling unsatisfied, frustrated and terribly *empty*.

Luckily for Rusty, God had let him into the secret that whilst his girl's more than willing pussy was *strictly* out of bounds until their wedding night, that didn't mean that he couldn't take his pleasures in any other way he saw fit. And so, a few nights after her eighteenth birthday, young Master McCloud had popped Alyssa's anal cherry, sating his appetite for penetration whilst still woefully neglecting her need for the same. Still, it had been pleasurable for Alyssa, and a most welcome change from Rusty's incessant frottering on her thighs, between her butt cheeks and over her breasts –

Rusty was especially fond of Alyssa's oily tit-jobs, he'd even spent some of his allowance on strawberry scented lubricant for that express purpose. To have Rusty's dick actually *inside* her body, to feel him swallowed up by her own hot flesh, was a delight, even if it was like torment from the Devil himself to have that delicious cock so close to her vagina; so close, but yet so infuriatingly far away.

Rusty had brought along a bottle of extra-special lubricant that first night - the label on the clear bottle even bragged that it was the number one lube for anal penetration - making it blatantly obvious to Alyssa as to exactly what he was expecting from her, she really didn't have much of a say in the matter.

Rusty had bought the stuff off of the internet of course – comically too embarrassed to walk in to *Walgreen's* and buy a bottle of sex lubricant, but not too embarrassed to assume his girlfriend would be more than happy to take his fat, stumpy cock in her virgin ass. To make matters worse, he'd bought a brand that went by the dubious name of *Pussy Juice* and was purported to feel – and smell – just like the real thing. This in particular Alyssa had found most insulting; if the boy was that hell-bent on realism, why in God's name didn't he just stick his cock in her vagina and have done with it?!

Oh yeah, the answer, as the man said, was right there in the question.

The lube had nonetheless piqued Alyssa's curiosity. She'd had a little experience with one of her girlfriends – she and Janey Seagrove had once gone as far as to compare and rub bare boobs in the changing rooms at the water park *and* had masturbated in front of each other during a sleepover. That had been a night to remember, seeing her best friend's naked body all sweaty and contorted as she came hard with three fingers crammed inside her sodden pussy, whilst Alyssa had rubbed frantically at her own clit, amazed at just how aroused and *squishy* her vagina had become simply by watching Janey's efforts. And although she had so desperately wanted to that night, Alyssa had never gone so far as to touch (let alone *taste*) Janey's pussy, nor any other than her own.

And so, intrigued by Rusty's *Pussy Juice* lube, which did actually smell a lot like warm, ripe pussy, Alyssa had squirted a little in her mouth to taste it.

Somewhat disappointingly, the stuff had tasted *nothing* like its namesake – certainly nothing at all like the salty-sweet, piscine flavor of Alyssa's own juices; instead the slippery liquid had carried the bitter tang of something nasty and industrial. It was actually something more akin to the stuff her father used to get the grease off of his hands when he'd been working on the Corvette (and yes, she'd tasted *that* too, albeit back when she was five and her big brother had convinced her it was lime *Jello*).

Of course Rusty had reassured Alyssa that she would enjoy anal sex, that God himself had decreed that this was how they should declare their physical love from now on. This of course precluded any and all protests from Alyssa, since the green light on her previously untouched orifice had been given by the Big Man himself, and she couldn't help but wonder if he'd be watching her maiden attempts at sodomy from up high on his cloud - and if so, would he be getting off on it?

And so, without much further ado Rusty rolled Alyssa over on the bed she'd slept in since the age of twelve when a summer growth spurt had shot her height up to five feet six inches and she'd sprouted pretty impressive breasts practically overnight, and squirted what felt to her like a gallon of *Pussy Juice* all over and between her buttocks. It still made Alyssa shudder to recall the chill of the fleshy-smelling lubricant as it splashed against the warm, round flesh of her pert butt cheeks, and how it trickled slowly into the cute crack that separated them to nudge at her puckered, brown rose like a persistent, icy finger. It had been not entirely unpleasant, as it turned out, especially once the warmth of her body heated the stuff up. Then the bottled *Pussy Juice* had made Alyssa feel so lasciviously wanton and *slippery*.

Rusty had stripped off his pants and boxers in record time and positioned himself between Alyssa's spread thighs. She'd felt his warm, strong hands grip her buttocks in order to prise them apart and she'd felt a tingle deep inside her belly at knowing that he had an uninterrupted view of her ass and (hopefully) her tight, pink pussy hole too. And a part of Alyssa hoped – *prayed* – somewhat ironically that Rusty may just miss and accidentally plunge his fat cock deep in to her vagina instead.

But no, Rusty's aim was true. And with much urgency and very little finesse, he'd pressed the bulging, purple head of his dick against the tightly resisting knot of her butt and rocked his hips and it felt as if the thing was actually knocking to be let in.

It had taken all of Alyssa's resolve – and a goodly amount of concentration – to relax her body enough to allow Rusty the entry to her rear that he so desired. In the end, she'd simply willed her muscles to relax, although they seemed determined at first to prevent any kind of ingress, but after five minutes or so of Rusty's relentless and most persistent prodding and Alyssa's relaxing, she'd felt the hard-yet-rubbery tip of his penis slide past the tight rim of her sphincter.

Alyssa had yelped at the surprising suddenness of that penetration, at the unexpected combined twinges of pain and pleasure at the invasion of her body and her ass had gripped so hard onto Rusty's cock - like she was trying to pull the thing from his body by its root. Naturally, Rusty had taken that as a sign that his best gal was having the time of her life and in one fell swoop he'd plunged his cock all the way down to its base in Alyssa's stretched asshole.

Her cry at that was altogether different. The pain had been so incredibly intense – the pleasure too – and had it not been for the liberal amounts of *Pussy Juice* that had made her entire nether regions sopping wet and slimy, Alyssa was convinced her clumsy boyfriend might well have caused some damage.

Then they'd each found their rhythm, rocking their bodies in perfect unison as Rusty's not insubstantial dick slid in and out of Alyssa's ass; him groaning with the sheer pleasure of actually fucking something, her moaning into the bed sheets at the wonderful *full* sensation that spread through her butt and the delightful tugging that Rusty's thrusting made on her swollen pussy lips and clit.

Rusty had climaxed pretty quickly as the tightness of Alyssa's body had stimulated his penis to the point of no return in record time. With a loud, animal grunt, he'd shot his thick wad of cum deep inside her rectum, and Alyssa was convinced she'd actually *felt* it splashing against the tender walls in there. He'd held his dick inside of her for a moment or two, as if reluctant to leave, but eventually Alyssa had felt Rusty's erection deflate and he slopped out of her ass amidst slick bubbles of lubricant and the sharp, tart smell of semen.

From that day forth, Rusty had always referred to Alyssa's ass as *God's Hole* and he simply couldn't get enough of it.

That was until Alyssa had accidentally found out that her boyfriend since ninth grade, the love of her life, the one she was saving herself for, had been slipping it to Pastor Shepherd's slutty daughter all along; for some reason the Good Lord had been okay with Rusty deflowering that particular dirty little hussy's vag', a fact that Alyssa had found particularly hard to swallow.

And that had been pretty much that. Alyssa had fought back the tears and packed Rusty off with a slapped face and his bottle of *Pussy Juice* - she had never spoken to the jerk since.

All those wasted years when she could have been enjoying being fucked properly, all the missed opportunities to have her *own* pussy juice lubricating bulging, teenaged cocks as they slid between her engorged lips and deep, deep down into her vagina. It was enough to make a gal go crazy.

Hence the overnight switch to the revealing, slutty clothes she'd always coveted when her friends wore them, and the unhesitating jump at the opportunity when she'd read the ad' for a surrogate who – would you believe it – *had* to be a virgin.

"Of course there'll be tests to determine your – *suitability*," the doctor's smooth, mellifluous voice broke in to Alyssa's reminiscing and she realized she'd only actually half heard what he'd been saying to her.

"Of course," Alyssa nodded her agreement. "I have no way of knowing for sure if I'm fertile or not, what with being a – err, with not ever having…" Alyssa stammered, unaccustomed to discussing such delicate, personal matters, even with a doctor. *Especially* with one so damned attractive that she was struggling to think much beyond liberating the cock she fantasized would be huge and magnificent from within his tight his pants and wriggling her sodden pussy down on to it like a wanton bitch in heat.

"My periods are regular," she told him and her cheeks flushed. "And there's no history of infertility on my mother's side." Alyssa forced a strained laugh as her attempted joke fell somewhat flat – despite his almost impossible handsomeness, the good doctor appeared to have had a sense of humor bypass.

The doctor leaned forward and laced his hands beneath his chin. "That's what we're here for," he said as he smiled at Alyssa and instantly she was pleased to be sitting down; his was a warm, welcoming smile that could easily have caused her knees to give way had she been standing. The doctor leaned forward a little more, his eyes scanning the length and breadth of Alyssa's body and beneath his delectable scrutiny she really hoped that she wasn't leaving a damp patch on his expensive chair. "There's nothing for you to worry about, my dear, I'm sure you will be just perfect."

His face fell serious – but still dangerously attractive – as he inhaled deeply through flared nostrils and Alyssa couldn't help but feel as if the dishy young doctor was actually *sniffing* her.

Suddenly, the doctor stood up. He pushed his chair backwards on its tiny wheels. And for a split second, Alyssa thought – *hoped* – that he was going to leap over the desk that separated them, thrust his hands up her woefully inadequate mini skirt and finger her slick, wanton pussy till she came hard and screamed the entire clinic down.

Alas no.

"I'll give you a few minutes to get undressed, Miss Bowers," the doctor said, much to Alyssa's disappointment – she was *really* longing for those long, lithe fingers on her clit right now – as he walked around his desk and made his way towards the door. "There's a gown on the hook for you. When you're done, if you could just make yourself comfortable on the couch, there are a few preliminary examinations we need to carry out."

"Okay," Alyssa replied as the doctor left the room and left her all alone.

Alyssa pulled her halter up and off over her head and immediately her petite rose colored nipples stood to attention in the cool, overly air conditioned room. The chill felt quite delicious on Alyssa's taut, puckered flesh and it sent an electric tingle through her body that made its way slowly but surely to somewhere deep inside her pussy.

Next she wriggled out of her skirt, letting it drop around her bare ankles. She kicked it away – along with her shoes – and looked down at the virginal panties that were all that now stood between her and being totally nude in the doctor's office. For a split second, Alyssa wondered if she was supposed to keep the panties on, and then smirked at her own foolishness; given the very nature of her business here, she figured that underwear would be more than surplus to requirements.

Alyssa slipped her underpants down over her silky thighs, relishing the soft caress of the white cotton against her bare legs – it felt just as she imagined the young doctor's tongue might feel were he to lick his way across her tingling skin on his way up to the moist, pink flesh of her pussy. Alyssa stroked lightly at the place she visualized the doctor's lips would kiss her tender flesh, running her fingers upwards towards the freshly trimmed fluff that nestled warmly between her thighs. With a sigh – and before she knew what she was doing (or *where* she was doing it) - Alyssa's fingers rested upon the dampness of her mound, one tip resting upon the swollen nub of her clit.

Parting her legs just a tad, Alyssa probed between her lips, marvelling at the hot slickness that greeted her; she really couldn't remember the last time she'd been this wet – certainly never with Rusty, unless it had been with the help of copious amounts of his ever-insulting *Pussy Juice*. She stared across the doctor's desk and imagined that the doctor was still sitting there, watching her play with herself as his hand stroked his rigid cock as she fingered her wet pussy for him. At that thought, Alyssa's free hand made its way to her breasts, kneading the pliant mounds, tweaking at the deliciously jutting nipples, and all the while Alyssa pretended that she was putting on a show for the hottest doctor in town.

"Oh," Alyssa murmured as she ventured a pair of fingers in to the tightness of her vagina, delighting in how her muscles clenched around them to suck the exploring digits in to her body. Across the virginal Rusty years, Alyssa and her fingers had become most intimately acquainted, and whilst they were scant substitution for a good, hard, pussy-stretching cock, they most certainly knew how to get the job done. Alyssa melted at the delectable sensation of the wriggling, moving things inside her body as those expert fingertips homed in on her G-spot whilst on the outside, her thumb pressed gently but oh so firmly upon her twitching clitoris.

And so, standing before her imaginary audience of one, Alyssa began to work in earnest at her pussy and tits, the frisson of the doctor's potential return to his office adding to her excitement – just *imagine* the look on his face if he caught her naked and masturbating like some naughty little schoolgirl in his office! Alyssa bent her knees a little more, parting her pussy lips and allowing her fingers to delve just a tad deeper inside her hole. By now her entire hand was dripping wet, soaked through with her slick, slippery juices as it worked its magic upon her sex.

Sensing that orgasm wasn't too far behind, Alyssa wilfully forced herself to clamp her mouth tight shut; she was apt to scream at times such as this, and that was an embarrassment she really could do well without. Her fingers danced frantically inside the wet, crinkled walls of her vagina, her thumb circling the head of her clit like she was trying to erase it and the pressure of a thundering climax drove Alyssa quickly and with urgency towards beautiful – and merciful – release.

Alyssa came hard against her hand, her internal muscles squeezing down on her fingers with such intensity that she felt her knuckles pop inside her pussy. She stifled the breathy moan that had built up behind her lips and dug her fingernails hard into the supple flesh of her breast, an action that served only to heighten her pleasure.

And then she was done.

Alyssa's orgasm flickered out like a spent match and Alyssa stood there, knees trembling through exertion and sodden fingers buried deep inside the moist heat of her vagina.

"Sweet Jesus," Alyssa groaned to herself, sliding her fingers out from her pussy, their movement triggering another pleasurable aftershock that rippled through her sweat-dampened body. Remembering where she was, and that Doctor Dishy would be back any moment, she looked around for the gown he'd told her was hanging on a hook somewhere.

And that's when she saw him.

"Good afternoon, Alyssa," the tall man by the door said, his voice soft, yet with a gravely undertone. "It is a pleasure to meet you." He smiled down at Alyssa and held out a hand for the shaking.

Alyssa stood, dumbfounded and quite noticeably naked. She stared blankly up at the man she recognized immediately. She'd seen his face on TV, on the cover of numerous magazines – *Time* and *National Geographic* to name but two, and all over the business pages of the *New York Times*. It was none other than Brett Wolfram, owner of the global phenomenon that was Wolfram International Industries, advisor to presidents, acclaimed philanthropist - and for some reason he was standing in a doctor's office in a clinic that his company owned watching a naked, twenty-two-year-old virgin bringing herself off.

Alyssa made no attempt to cover her body, there really did seem to be little point, given the circumstances. Part of her mind screamed that she really ought to be embarrassed as hell and at least put an arm over her bare tits, but there was just something about the tall, olive-skinned man with the warm smile and expensive suit that put her so readily at ease. And so there Alyssa stood, as naked as the day she'd slipped kicking and screaming out of her mother's vagina, smiled and before she could help herself she was shaking hands with of one of the richest men on the planet with her cum-soaked hand.

"Oh, I am *so* sorry." Alyssa blanched as she pulled her glistening hand away from Wolfram's, mortified by the slick residue her fingers had left on his. Absently, she wiped her hand on her naked buttock, the juice cooling there on her exposed skin.

"Nothing to be sorry about, young lady," Wolfram cracked a smile and lifted his hand to somewhere just below his nose, inhaling deeply – just what was it with these people and *sniffing* things?

Alyssa watched the man intently, studying his tall, broad frame, his thick black hair, slightly hooked nose and dazzling teeth that were the perfect compliment to his impossibly handsome face. She tried to remember how old Wolfram was supposed to be; was it fifties, sixties even? It was impossible for her to tell, the man looked even younger than the toy boy her mother had hooked up with after

Dad had run away with Byron, his personal assistant – and that guy was barely into his thirties.

Of course, Alyssa had no way of knowing just how long the billionaire had been standing behind her, nor any idea as to how he had gotten in to the doctor's office without her knowing – the room wasn't that big that she wouldn't have noticed someone coming in, even if she was jilling herself senseless. Just how much of her performance had he seen? Clearly she didn't dare ask, and Wolfram seemed too polite to say anything, so Alyssa figured it safe to assume that she'd just masturbated to a teeth-grinding, shuddering orgasm in front of him – whilst imagining the gorgeous doctor sitting in his chair jerking off to her actions.

"You are just *perfect*," Wolfram said, his voice deep and masterful.

"Pardon me?" Alyssa stepped towards him, shoulders back and heaving breasts thrust towards the man, as if begging for him to grasp them roughly in those huge hands of his and tug at her nipples with those strong (wet!) fingers until she came once more.

"For bearing my child," Wolfram told her, as matter of fact as if he were offering Alyssa some menial office job. "That's why you are here?"

"Err – yes," Alyssa stammered, thinking that otherwise this situation could *really* have been deemed awkward. "That's *exactly* why I'm here." She attempted a smile as Wolfram cast his dark eyes over her nude body, and she was amazed at how much at ease the man had put her. There was just something in those dark, hypnotic eyes that soothed her, made her aware of her nakedness but not in the least bit ashamed of the fact - and Alyssa simply loved the tiny flecks of gold in those deep brown irises that reminded her of those ludicrously expensive gold leaf cocktails Rusty had always insisted on buying for her on her birthday.

Wolfram turned on his heels, his bespoke Italian shoes squeaking on the tiled floor. He pulled open the door and in the beat of a heart, Alyssa was once more alone and so undeniably nude in the doctor's office.

He met the doctor out in the hallway. The doctor bustled towards him with a harassed look on his face.

"She will do perfectly, have her prepared and sent to the house," Wolfram instructed.

The doctor stared nervously at the tall, imposing man and said quietly, "But, the tests – "

"I said…" Wolfram insisted, leaning towards the doctor, his considerable height towering still further over the man, his formidable shadow darkening the medic's white coat.

"I'll see to it straight away." The doctor offered a weak grin to show that he was *absolutely delighted* with his orders; it was a grin that convinced neither Wolfram, nor himself.

Chapter Two

Wolfram's house, as it turned out, was a vast, sprawling, Seventeenth Century mansion in the middle of a huge expanse of forest in some far flung Eastern European country that Alyssa had never heard of, let alone had any chance of pronouncing; far too many consonants, too few vowels for her liking.

She was ferried in style from Wolfram's private jet at the private airport – no lines, no intrusive TSA scans - by a long, black limousine that had plush, cream-colored leather seats and a mini bar. Of course, the bar was stocked only with soft drinks only – no alcohol for the surrogate-to-be!

Alyssa was met at the formidable front door to Wolfram's house – solid oak adorned with fat, metal studs; three hundred years old and almost a foot thick – by a rather stern but immensely attractive woman who Alyssa guessed to be forty something if she was a day. She had classically handsome features, the blackest hair and an incredible body beneath a tight fitting black dress that stopped mid-thigh to show off beautifully toned legs. There was just something in the way in which the woman walked, something about the gentle lilt of her accent, something about that tight, perfect body that created a tiny ache of longing deep between Alyssa's legs and Alyssa couldn't help but wonder what the woman's pussy might taste like.

Oblivious to Alyssa's most uncharacteristic and incredibly lascivious thoughts, the woman courteously but coldly introduced herself as the *Mistress of the House* and without ceremony ushered Alyssa into and through the place and directly up to her designated suite.

"Mr. Wolfram is out hunting," the Mistress informed Alyssa. "He will be back to see you later."

"Hunting?" Alyssa was not a big fan of blood sports; she even thought it cruel when her father went fishing. "He's allowed to hunt off-season here?"

"Mr Wolfram can do as he pleases on his own land," the Mistress replied with a cold, detached expression.

"He owns the *whole* forest?"

"He owns the whole country," the Mistress informed her, and this time Alyssa thought she caught the faint glimmer of a smile on the woman's infinitely kissable, plump lips. And she couldn't help but wonder what those lips would feel like clamped down tight against her pussy whilst the Mistress's tongue made itself busy inside her hot, wet hole.

Somewhere in the distant background, possibly off in some far flung wing of the gigantic house, a dog barked. Its voice was joined by another, and then a couple more and soon Alyssa was listening to their harsh, baying chorus as if it were the ideal soundtrack to her surreal adventure.

After what had seemed like an age, the two arrived at Alyssa's quarters. The Mistress sashayed in through the thick oak door and Alyssa was unable to take her eyes off of the woman's round, peachy ass and tried her damndest to take her mind off the growing damp spot in her own panties.

"You'll find everything you need here," the Mistress said. "If you *do* need anything else, just ask." She pointed to the phone on the nightstand by the mammoth four-poster bed that dominated the room.

"I will, thank you," Alyssa told her, and it flitted across her mind to say that the one thing she needed right now was the Mistress's fingers buried deep inside her vagina and those full, luscious lips sucking frantically at her clit.

But before Alyssa could make any such request, the Mistress of the House had turned on her shapely heels and vacated the room. The door closed behind her with a solid, resounding *clunk* and Alyssa found herself all alone in the magnificent suite in Brett Wolfram's ridiculously large house.

The suite comprised the main room – which contained the bed that was so spacious that Alyssa feared she may actually get lost in it – a sitting room with a massive picture window that looked out onto the forest and the tiny dots of light that glowed from the village down in the valley, and a roomy, luxurious bathroom decked in solid marble and complete with a claw foot tub big enough for at least two good-sized individuals that stood dead center in the room. Alyssa began to smile at that thought, and entertained the fleeting idea that perhaps the Mistress might be along later to help her try the tub out for size – but then Alyssa remembered her one reason for being at the house, in this suite, and her smile faded.

*

It was much later – by now it was pitch black outside and the forest beyond Alyssa's window was lit only by the slivery glow of the full moon and the sprinkling of stars in the night sky – when Wolfram finally made an appearance. Alyssa was dressed for bed and had just finished the dinner Mistress had ordered up for her - the thickest, rarest steak that Alyssa thought she'd ever laid eyes upon and vegetables so damned fresh she could practically taste the sweet, earthy tones of dirt – when she heard a polite knock upon her door.

"Come in," Alyssa said as she dabbed the last of the bloodied steak juice from the corners of her mouth, and felt more than a little awkward upon saying that when Wolfram entered the room – this was *his* house, after all.

"I see that you have settled in." Wolfram smiled an incredibly warm, *gentle* smile and parked himself upon the old, leather couch next to Alyssa. The couch creaked under his tall, muscular frame and Alyssa caught a whiff of the guy's no doubt terribly expensive cologne.

"I have, thank you," Alyssa said. "This place is awesome."

"Consider it your home," Wolfram told her, and again that smile, "for as long as you wish."

At this, Wolfram eased his huge frame forwards on the couch, placed his elbows on his knees and laced his fingers in front of his face. A serious look settled on his handsome features and those sparkling gold flecks in his eyes twinkled at Alyssa.

At once, Alyssa felt incredibly conscious of the fact that she was in a foreign land she could scarcely pronounce, a million miles from home and everyone she knew, sitting in a suite fit for royalty whilst dressed in a short, white cotton nightgown through which the dark pink of her nipples could easily be seen – in the presence of the incredibly powerful Brett Wolfram. She felt the icy spread of gooseflesh crawling over her body and she felt so woefully *exposed.*

"We must make time to discuss the finer points of our arrangement," Wolfram said, his voice calm, soothing. "And please do remember that you are free to leave here at any time."

Alyssa looked around the room, tasted the rich, bloody flavor of the steak upon her tongue and thought she'd *never* want to leave, not under any circumstances.

"Although you are to remain here following insemination *and* for the duration of your pregnancy; so you may receive the very best medical care, of course."

Alyssa nodded, she had in point of fact read that part of the contract, but not much else – the size of the paycheck attached to the thick sheaf of papers had clouded her vision pretty much after that paragraph and she'd not been able to sign the papers quick enough.

"And with regards to the insemination itself," Wolfram's voice dipped, as if in a rare moment of embarrassment. "That is to be carried out in the – *traditional* way."

"Pardon me?" Alyssa plucked her glass of water from the TV tray, gulped down the icy liquid so quickly that it gave her a slight brain freeze. She most certainly couldn't remember reading *that* in the contract, and had naturally assumed that the whole affair would be all sterile clinics, stirrups and turkey basters. But no, if she was hearing Brett Wolfram correctly, he was entirely expecting to fuck her.

"I'm sorry, I've offended you," Wolfram said, his voice cool and professional – more as if he were in some delicate business negotiation and not announcing that he was about to fuck a girl *at least* half his age. "It was in the contract –"

"I'm sorry - I guess I must have missed that part." Alyssa smiled at the man, her eyes studying his gorgeous features; his toned, broad body, his strong, masterful hands and those infinitely hypnotic eyes.

"Ah," Wolfram made as if to stand up.

"It's okay." Alyssa surprised herself; she'd never been one to make snap decisions. She placed a hand on Wolfram's thigh, felt the thick, taught muscles tensing there and she figured *what the hell.* "I'd be happy to fuck you." Again, she surprised herself, she'd never – *ever* – said such a thing to a man before, especially one as powerful and with a bank account that could easily clear the national debt of several small countries.

"Like I said, Miss Bowers, you are free to leave – "

"I won't be leaving," Alyssa assured him; amused as to how the tables seemed to have turned and that now she appeared to be the one in the driving seat. She ran her hand along his thigh, aiming for the delicious looking bulge in his crotch, all the time wondering how big his cock would be and what it would feel like stuffed to the hilt inside her aching virgin pussy. "I guess you'd like to get started then?"

"There will be plenty of time for that later," Wolfram said, firmly yet politely. He placed a hand on top of hers to effectively – and frustratingly - prevent her further progress towards his nether regions. "Virginity is not something to be taken – or given – lightly." He stood up from the couch.

Alyssa sat there in dumbfounded silence. He'd actually said *no*, albeit with impeccable politeness – another first for her; Rusty had never been one to turn down a BJ or *Pussy Juice* playtime in God's Hole. At once, she felt incredibly special, and although there was the most pleasurable throbbing through the walls of her rapidly moistening pussy, Alyssa knew that losing her virginity to Wolfram would be well worth waiting for.

"Get yourself some rest, enjoy our hospitality, and feel free to explore a little." Wolfram was once again back in control of the situation, although Alyssa could see the effect she'd had on the man – the front of his pants were quite noticeably tented, as if some wild animal were trying to burst out from the expensive material.

And then he was gone. The door swung closed behind him and Alyssa found herself once more all alone and contemplating the fact that she'd just agreed to fuck one of the most powerful men on the planet.

Then, an oddly out of place noise filtered through the thick walls; it sounded to Alyssa to be the muffled sound of voices, of laughter and it more than aroused Alyssa's interest. So, despite the colossal plasma TV bolted to the bare brick wall opposite her massive – and unbelievably uncomfortable - bed, and the untold number of channels at her disposal, Alyssa was in no mood to sit still, even this late at night - her mind was already racing full steam ahead, her pussy aching with anticipation.

Venturing out of her suite with her mouth dry and heat thumping, Alyssa felt a little like a wayward boarding school girl off to raid the pantry, keep to sample the clandestine delights of the teacher's secret pantry. The hallway beyond her room was long and draughty, its slate tiled floor chilly beneath her bare feet, as if it were sucking her body heat out from her soles. A cool breeze swirled by, wafting around her naked thighs, tickling her clit with long, icy fingers and Alyssa was so pleased that she had eschewed panties beneath the flimsy nightdress – the fresh air cavorting around her nude pussy made her feel so mouth-wateringly *naughty*.

After what seemed to be an age slinking through the Wolfram mansion's dim corridors, Alyssa came upon a room at the very end of a narrow hallway that ran off at a right-angle from the main one. The noises she'd first heard way back in her suite appeared to be coming from within, and judging by the sounds of lascivious laughter, whoever was beyond that particular metal-studded door was having much more fun than watching *NCIS* reruns.

With a furtive glance behind her, and filled with the feeling that she really ought not to be there, Alyssa eased open the door, breathing a sigh of relief that it had been left cracked open just a tad.

What met Alyssa's eyes did little to ease the ravenous craving that ached deep down in her loins and made her swollen pussy lips slick and slippery wet.

The room beyond the door was cavernous, the bare stone walls lit only by myriad fat, white, flickering candles. The floor, like the walls, was dark, unadorned stone, and in the dead centre of the room there sat an immense bed – easily as big as four of hers pushed together – draped with thick, black sheets.

There appeared to be two dozen or so people around the bed, an even mix of male and female. All were in their early twenties, their beautiful young bodies naked and entirely untouched by time and gravity; the girls were lithe, firm and with beautifully proportioned breasts, the young men spectacularly broad chested, incredibly toned and with long, eagerly jutting cocks.

The male contingent, Alyssa noted, appeared to bear more than a passing resemblance to Wolfram, even down to the gold flecks in their eyes that sparked as they reflected the dancing candlelight. They also seemed to be some dressed up as wild animals – bizarre looking, hairy, lupine things.

Alyssa guessed that she was witnessing some kind of kinky role play - who knew what the norm was in this strange land? She'd heard before about people who dressed up as all kinds of animals to get their kicks – some even wore stuffed animal costumes as part of their peculiar kink! And whilst she did struggle to understand the *why*, there was no escaping the fact that she was finding the whole scene playing out before her to be undeniably and unavoidably erotic.

Two alabaster skinned, large breasted girls knelt in the center of the bed. They were kissing each other hungrily with wide, open mouths and probing tongues that would occasionally escape, slipping out from the sensual seal like pink, slippery wild creatures. The girls' hands kneaded one another's tits, tweaking nipples, digging long fingernails into the pliant flesh so as to leave pink, glowing crescents upon the smooth skin. And as Alyssa watched, rapt, the girls in unison snaked a hand down to the other's smoothly denuded pudendum, wriggling fingers quickly parting the puffy lips there to make their way deep inside hot, wet vaginas.

As the girls sighed in their shared ecstasy, one of the young men clambered between them, and standing on the bed he slipped his long, thick cock between their kissing mouths. Both girls welcomed the dick eagerly, slurping at it with plump lips, lapping at it with lively tongues; fighting over who was to be the first one to draw the delectable meat deep into their greedy mouth.

Two more men joined the three, their dicks rock solid and standing firm at that jutting, urgent forty-five-degree angle from their bodies, pointing persistently at the white-skinned girls like little kids in a toy store. One of the men positioned behind one of the girls, the other behind the other, and they each meandered an exploratory hand beneath their respective choice, accompanying the girl's fingers inside their spread pussies, digits entwining within the tight, sodden vaginas.

Other pairings joined the affray on the bed; a guy and a girl, two girls, two guys and one girl, two girls and one guy – and as Alyssa watched, they all kind of merged into one mass of sweat-glistening skin, frantic mouths, pumping cocks, spread thighs and slick, pink pussies. She saw fingers thrusting deep inside mouths and vaginas and asses, tongues lapping up juices and sweat, cocks plunging in and out of holes, pulling flesh taut and slapping wetly against buttocks and thighs and round, plump tits.

Unable to help herself, Alyssa allowed a hand to wander down to her own pussy, not in the least surprised to find it volcanically hot down there. Her fingers slipped between her engorged labia with slick ease as she sought out the aching nub of her clitoris.

A movement caught Alyssa's eye from within the room. A new couple approached the bed; eyes alight with absolute animal lust as they watched the writhing, fucking heap of flesh that awaited them. The girl was petite with a perfect hourglass figure and firm, jiggling breasts with high, dark nipples. Her hips swayed beautifully as she walked hand in hand with her chosen man, her pouting pussy lips parting slightly as she did so to allow the delicate folds of her inner labia to peek suggestively through. Her man was as white skinned and epilated as she, a stark contrast to the hairy young men upon the bed, his cock erect and pressed against his belly, its dark pink head bobbing rhythmically as he walked.

Alyssa probed inside her vagina with two lively, wiggling fingers, doing her very best to sate the craving that gnawed within and trying to imagine what it must be like for the girls on the bed to be penetrated and *filled* by the girth of the enormous pricks that parted their lips and disappeared deep inside their willing young bodies. She slipped her fingers out of her pussy and applied their slick dexterity to her clit, rubbing it hard with long, deliberate strokes, so hard that she had to bite down hard on her lower lip to stifle the moan that threatened to spill out from her mouth and give her voyeurism away.

Caught up in her own masturbation, Alyssa barely registered the subtle change in the young man who stood by the bed as if a tad overwhelmed at just where he was supposed to start. His once smooth skin appeared to be darkening, his tall stature hunching over just a little, his chest broadened. The young man's face looked to Alyssa to be twisting out of shape, elongating almost - although Alyssa's pleasure-soaked brain chalked that up to the movement of the flickering candles and the long, shifting shadows that they cast across the absolute decadence of the orgy.

And as Alyssa came against her hand she clamped her thighs as tight together as she had her mouth to prevent herself from screaming out loud as a powerful orgasm raced through her shuddering body, the young man climbed on to the bed. He guided the woman behind him with a hand that now had long, spindly fingers and what appeared to be black, curved claws. His body was now as hirsute as those of the other men, his long, masterful cock stiff and proud and so obviously eager to be buried deep inside the hot wet flesh that was presented to it, his face pinched and pointed like a kid's Halloween mask. And then those gold flecked eyes glanced up and for a brief moment they locked with Alyssa's.

"You should be resting," a voice from behind made Alyssa jump almost from her damp, glowing skin. Startled, she spun around to meet the stern gaze of the Mistress.

"I-I'm sorry, I was just – "

"I can see what you were doing," the Mistress said with a downward glance. Awkwardly, Alyssa realized that she still had her fingers squeezed between her legs, their tips resting upon her tingling clit.

"This is not for you," the Mistress informed Alyssa, reaching by her to pull the door shut. "You are for the Master only, when you are ready."

"I think I'm ready now," Alyssa groaned as she prised her hand from her pussy. It came away wet and glistening.

"Then your time will be tomorrow," the Mistress advised with little emotion in her voice. "We will have you suitably prepared."

And as she allowed herself to be led back to her room by the severe yet incredibly hot older woman, Alyssa's mind raced with myriad thoughts of what she was convinced she'd just witnessed inside the orgy room, although already she was beginning to doubt herself.

Chapter Three

They came the next evening to prepare her.

Alyssa had spent most of the day sleeping, flicking absently through the TV channels and picking at the gourmet food the Mistress had delivered to her room by several of the pale-skinned, full breasted beauties she was positive she'd recognized from the night before at the strange orgy.

Alyssa had not dared to venture again from the confines of her suite, not after the icy, forbidding look the Mistress had given her the night before upon returning her to her room and bidding her a *very good night*. The woman had said nothing more – hadn't *needed* to – her eyes had let Alyssa know in no uncertain terms that she was to stay put in future, and to not poke her nose around in things she had no party to – no matter how tempting they may seem.

The twin girls sent to prepare Alyssa were young, she guessed them to be around the same age as the pair playing with each other's dripping pussies on the bed Alyssa had fingered herself to the night before. At first Alyssa had thought that it *was* them, but as they disrobed the minute they'd entered her room, Alyssa saw straight away that these two were heavy with child, their round bellies distended and swollen, and their breasts engorged with milk.

"We must bathe you," one of the girls informed her – it was impossible for Alyssa to tell them apart; both had long, black, silken hair, milky complexions and perfectly symmetrical faces with full, luscious blood-red lips – and they both led Alyssa by her hands into the spacious bathroom. In turn they smiled at Alyssa and slipped her nightdress up over her head so that she was as naked as they were.

"If you would care to step in to the tub," the other girl purred, "we shall begin."

Unquestioning, Alyssa stepped in to the empty bathtub, its cast iron bottom freezing cold against the bare soles of her feet. As a kid, she'd always been taught to put the water in the tub first - to ensure the temperature was *just* right - before getting into a bath. Still, this was a strange country, where she'd seen strange things, and this was by far way down on her *strange* list.

Although not for long, as it transpired.

Alyssa reclined in the empty tub, doing her best to think warm thoughts and ignore the chill from its metal sides that nipped at her naked flesh. She draped a protective arm across her breasts to hide what she could, while her other she rested against the wispy hair that surrounded her pussy. This seemed to amuse the two girls no end, as they were most unashamedly naked in Alyssa's presence, their full tits jiggling and bare feet slapping on the tiled floor as they circled the tub like vultures circling their prey.

"A little warm water would be appreciated," Alyssa said, gooseflesh rising all over her body - bare toes to scalp.

The girls ignored her. They positioned themselves either side of the tub and looked down at Alyssa's naked body with a far away look in their beautiful brown eyes. Then, they began to stroke their breasts.

Alyssa watched, mesmerised as the twins massaged those full, malleable mounds of flesh that were topped with broad, dark pink nipples that she guessed must have been almost a full inch long. And there was just something so delectably sensual about the pregnant girls' kneading of their breasts that made Alyssa want to dig her fingers in to her own and grind them against her ribcage until she could stand it no longer.

When the first fine spray of warmth alighted on Alyssa's body it took her completely by surprise. She let out a small, breathy gasp as she felt the hot liquid settle on her soft, sensitive skin between her tits and trickle down her cleavage. Without thinking, she moved the arm that concealed her nipples, desperately longing to feel the warmth of the liquid on the pink buds that stiffened at that very thought.

More of the warm fluid sprayed her body, and Alyssa looked up at the girls who were standing over her and saw thin sprays of milk squirting out from their nipples, mingling mid air and falling like sweet, sensual rain over Alyssa's naked, reclining body.

"Oh my," Alyssa moaned as her body grew shiny and wet with the sticky breast milk of the lactating twins. They smiled their benign smile down at her and leaned towards each other, each one placing their hands upon their opposite's tits. The milk now flowed thick and free from their huge mounds, each sister's expert hands coaxing the gushing white liquid from heavy, sensual breasts like milkmaids at a cow's udder, all the while drenching Alyssa head to toe.

Alyssa caressed her own body, rubbing the delectably smooth milk into her skin, relishing the feel of her bare breasts that were made slippery with milk, of her flat belly and navel in which pooled the sweet nectar. She lifted her face into the streams of milk, mouth wide, tongue protruding like a child catching snowflakes, and drank down the wonderful liquid like she'd never be able to get enough.

The twin girls ceased their mutual lactation and knelt either side of the tub. They reached for Alyssa's body and massaged their milk into her skin in much the same way as they had done to coax the precious fluid from themselves. Alyssa sighed and writhed beneath their touch, her disappointment that their milking had stopped giving way to the sensual caress of their strong, lithe fingers. Alyssa figured by then that she was laying in an inch or so of human milk – a truly amazing feat for the petite twins - its slightly sticky texture clinging to her skin, coating her, making her smell so incredibly debauched and feel so delightfully like a fuck-anything, wanton slut.

One of the twins parted Alyssa's legs, presenting her pussy for them both to see. They both gazed as if in awe at the plump, pouting lips between Alyssa's thighs and teased them apart with firm fingers to study the pink, glinting hole within. They looked at one another and nodded as if in approval.

A straight razor was produced, much to Alyssa's consternation; just where two naked chicks had concealed the thing was somewhat a mystery to her. She glanced down the length of her milk-slicked body at the razor that reminded her of the one her Grandpa used to shave off the rough, week's worth of stubble that clung to his rugged chin every Sunday morning before church, and wondered just why the dark haired twin holding it was manoeuvring the keen blade down towards her pussy.

Whilst one girl held the delicate skin around Alyssa's pussy stretched taut, the other ran the wickedly sharp razor over the fine down of her pubic hair. The liberal coating of breast milk from the lactating twins had rendered Alyssa's skin glossy and practically friction-free and her pussy fuzz fell quickly away to leave her pudendum sensuously bare and cool.

When they had finished shaving her, Alyssa couldn't help but reach down to touch the denuded skin with tentative fingertips; she'd never *completely* shaved down there before and had always wondered what it would feel like to have a totally naked quim. And now she knew – and it was mind blowing; Alyssa could feel even the lightest touch of her fingertips, as if her skin had suddenly sprouted a million more nerve endings – and she couldn't wait to feel her sire's body grinding against it.

They rinsed Alyssa off with water so warm that it made her skin glow a pleasant pink color. The milk from the pregnant girls' engorged breasts had left her entire body feeling smooth and so incredibly *cleansed* and she couldn't shake the thought that she had actually been *anointed* rather than simply bathed. Either way, this was the most amazing Alyssa could ever remember feeling; her every nerve ending felt as if it were alight and tingling, her pussy was sizzling hot, wet and tight, her libido cranked so high off the charts she imagined she could cum just by thinking about cumming. Surrogacy and financial agreement be damned, Alyssa was ready for some good ol' fashioned, hard core fucking!

The pregnant twins – still scrumptiously naked, their swollen, pendulous breasts swaying provocatively – dressed Alyssa in a gray nightshirt that fell to just below the curve of her buttocks and smelled unmistakably of *him*. They tied Alyssa's wrists together – loose but firm – in front of her and slipped a black, silk blindfold over her eyes, thus rendering her entirely at their mercy. And as they led her out from the suite and down along a seemingly endless maze of cold stone hallways, all Alyssa could think of was Wolfram's broad length of cock squeezing into her tight, virginal pussy until she was fit to burst.

They came at last to the wide, metal door to Wolfram's wing of the house. The chill metal clanged harshly as the pregnant twins heaved it open and its ancient hinges creaked their complaint with a harsh creaking sound that jabbed cruelly at Alyssa's heightening hearing.

"The Master is waiting for you," one of the girls whispered to Alyssa. "It is your time." She led Alyssa in to the room, which had a raw, smoky heat to it, and in the background Alyssa could hear the lazy crackling of an open log fire. And above the sour-sweet smell of the burning wood, Alyssa caught scent of something altogether more primal, something inherently *animal*.

They had Alyssa kneel down on what felt to her bare legs to be a thick pile rug, and Alyssa imagined it to be fashioned from a bear pelt – most likely one the preternaturally masculine Brett Wolfram had hunted down and killed up close and personal – possibly even one of those with the poor animal's head and fat, desiccated paws still attached to it. There she waited, listening to the soft *pad-pad-pad* of the twins' bare feet on the stone floor as they made their way back out of the room. They left and the door closed behind them with a loud, groaning screech and a resounding *clang*.

"Welcome, Miss Bowers," Wolfram's voice boomed across the room, making Alyssa jump a little at its suddenness. She heard movement behind her and instinctively cocked her head, certain she'd heard the faint rattling of chains. "I would like to apologize if you found the ritual of preparing you for this a little strange - our people have their customs, you see." Wolfram's voice inched ever closer as he spoke, his arousing accent more pronounced with each syllable.

"Don't mention it," Alyssa said, her own voice breathy with anticipation, her senses – and her sex – at their peak. "I really quite enjoyed it."

"That is important," Wolfram told her, so close behind her now that she could feel the moist heat of his breath on the nape of her neck. And suddenly, despite the loose fitting nightshirt that covered much of her naked, epilated body, Alyssa felt so incredibly *exposed*. "At the point of orgasm, the tip of the cervix dips down into the accumulated semen at the end of the vagina in order to scoop it up," Wolfram explained, sounding more like a fertility counsellor than a lover. "And that helps to ensure a successful impregnation. So you can understand why it is imperative that you enjoy all of this."

Alyssa nodded. With the way her sexual tension had been built up since her arrival at Wolfram's mansion, there was absolutely no way she *couldn't* enjoy what was to come.

She felt Wolfram's strong, muscular arms enfold her body, the tightness of his broad chest pressing against her back. His hands found her wrists and tugged at the thick velvet rope that bound them and again, she heard the metallic rattle of chains. Her wrists were soon free and Wolfram whispered gently in her ear that she may now remove her blindfold.

The first thing Alyssa saw as her eyes grew accustomed to the dim, candle lit room was the Mistress of the house standing quietly, patiently in one corner of the room, her slim body enshrouded by quivering shadows. The next, upon turning around, was that Wolfram himself wore nothing more than a fat, metal collar around his neck, from which snaked a chain that was anchored to a large steel hoop embedded in the gray stone wall.

"It's for your safety," the Mistress broke her silence.

"Why would I not be safe?" Alyssa asked, not as taken aback at the Mistress's presence as she thought she should be – in some perverse way she found it to be reassuring.

"Sometimes, these things can get a little out of hand," the Mistress told her. "Especially on a night such as this." She glanced towards the open window, the unforgiving light of the full moon sparkling in her eyes.

"And what if I don't *want* to be safe?" Alyssa was feeling incredibly bold; her desire to be ravished by the powerful Wolfram had overridden all common sense and shyness. "Perhaps I need to feel whatever danger you seem to be scared of in order to cum?"

"I really don't think – "

"Unchain him," Alyssa said, surprised at her own insistence.

"Are you sure that's what you want?" Wolfram stood to his full height, his formidable, semi-erect penis so tantalizingly close to Alyssa's face; one swift move and she knew she could have the thing in her mouth and be sucking upon it as one would a delicious and rare sweetmeat.

"I'm sure," Alyssa looked up into Wolfram's handsome face, disappointed at just how emasculated and powerless he looked chained up like some performing animal in a sad circus sideshow. If what she'd seen at the orgy the night before was to be any indication of what the great Brett Wolfram was, this was something Alyssa wanted more than anything in her life thus far.

"Do as she says," Wolfram instructed the Mistress.

The Mistress walked over from her corner with her face set stony in silent protest, her vertiginous, stiletto heels *click-clacking* on the stone floor. She produced an old, chunky metal key from her skirt pocket and undid the collar around Wolfram's neck.

Alyssa winced at the hollow, clattering noise the collar and its chain made as it cascaded to the floor.

She then looked up at Wolfram who stood tall, magnificently naked and once again infinitely powerful behind her.

"Leave us," Wolfram instructed the Mistress of the house.

Clearly, the woman was in no position to protest against Wolfram's wishes, and so she, too left the room.

Alyssa shivered against the cool breeze that filtered in through the open window, carrying with it the fresh scent of pine and rain dampened forest dirt. She felt a little more vulnerable with the Mistress's departure, yet it was a vulnerability that served only to further intensify her sense of arousal. She stood up to face Wolfram, her head at his chest height, her eyes soaking up the sheer beauty of the man. His body was wide and rippled with taut muscles that lurked beneath his unblemished olive skin - the suit he'd worn the first time they'd met at the clinic had only hinted at the perfection of the body beneath. She glanced down at those thick, strong legs that seemed to go on forever, and at the broad, lengthy cock that was now fully stiffened and everything she had dreamed it would be – and more.

Wolfram lowered his face towards Alyssa's and pressed his lips to hers. He kissed her firmly, masterfully and without the adolescent urgency that she had gotten so accustomed to with Rusty. Her lips parted at the gentle pressure of his and soon Alyssa felt a long and dominant tongue making its way into her mouth, seeking hers, caressing it, lapping from it. She felt Wolfram's hands stroking her flanks, making their way downwards to tug at the hem of her shirt, and with the briefest of breaks from their kiss, he'd pulled the flimsy garment up and over her head, discarding it amongst the chains upon the floor.

At last, Alyssa was completely and totally naked with Wolfram. She felt the heat from his body radiating into each and every one of her pores, warming her naked body, seeping deep into her flesh. Wolfram pulled her to him, their bodies pressed tight together, the hardness of his cock pushed into her belly, as if it wanted to implant its seed into her then and there from the outside – as if it couldn't wait to be squeezing its way into her pussy.

Wolfram broke the kiss, his tongue slipping with reluctance from her sucking, nibbling mouth, and he lay Alyssa down on the rug – she had been right, it was bear, although mercifully *sans* grinning, toothy head and dried up feet. Wolfram positioned himself over her supine, naked body. He lowered his head and lapped at the soft skin around Alyssa's firm, pouting nipples, circling each one in turn, wetting, teasing them so that they stood even more to attention. He took her left nipple between his lips, sucking it deep towards the back of his throat, stroking its sensitive skin with his tongue as it slipped inside the warmth of his mouth. Alyssa moaned as waves of pleasure washed over her, the intensity of the sensation in her breasts almost too much to bear. She buried her hands in the thick mat of her lover's hair and pressed him harder on to her tit.

He pulled away, leaving Alyssa's nipple wanting as he had done her tongue, and he danced his own tongue down along the deep crevasse of her cleavage and on towards her belly button. There he paused to dip his tongue into the sweet hollow, which sent a tingle through Alyssa's belly that she'd never experienced before. Wolfram then traced his tongue downwards from her navel, leaving a thin trail of cooling moisture in its wake and made its way over the gentle bump of her epilated mound and down between the soft folds of her pussy.

Alyssa moaned out loud and lifted her hips to meet Wolfram's probing tongue. She squirmed as it circled the bulging tip of her clit and expertly parted her inner lips to gain access to her sweet spot.

And then he was inside her.

Wolfram's long, muscular, slippery tongue penetrated the tight entrance to Alyssa's vagina and his mouth pressed tight against her sizzling flesh and Alyssa couldn't help but cry out as pleasure radiated out from her pussy and into every corner of her body. She lifted her head to better see the man who was so proficiently eating her out, to watch as his face moved so expertly between her thighs, his lips and cheeks glistening wet from her juices. She heard Wolfram grunting with appreciation and his own gratification as he licked and sucked and slurped at her most intimate place, and Alyssa thought that had to be the most sensual sound in the world.

As he revelled in the tastes and scent and texture of Alyssa's sopping, tight pussy, Wolfram's groans of ecstasy underwent a subtle change; they became ever deeper, the gravel in his voice more pronounced, almost more of a growl than a groan. Alyssa found this to be even *more* arousing - there was something inherently *animal* about the sounds Wolfram was making.

And as Alyssa watched, Brett Wolfram's body began to change.

Muffled as it was between Alyssa's spread legs, Wolfram's face began to elongate and she felt his tongue thicken inside of her – this elicited another sigh from her lips and she gripped his shoulders tightly with both hands, urging him on. There she felt the sudden coarseness of hair as it sprouted out from his skin like thousands of tiny snakes, writhing, growing ever longer as they coated his broad shoulders, their action mirrored the length of his magnificent body.

Wolfram's face now more resembled a snout, complete with pronounced muzzle and stiff, prickling whiskers that stabbed at the raw, pink flesh between Alyssa's pussy lips in a most tantalizing manner. He looked up into Alyssa's eyes and she saw that although he was now barely recognizable as Brett Wolfram, although his startling gold-flecked eyes remained and now they stared deep into hers with a look that was undeniably far more *beast* than man.

Wolfram pulled away from Alyssa's dripping vagina, the short fur on his face slicked down with her wetness, his glinting white teeth protruding ever so slightly in a decidedly canine grin.

Supporting himself on powerful forelegs and huge, clawed paws, Wolfram positioned himself over Alyssa, looking down upon her reclined, naked body with a look of pure, unadulterated lust. His cock, she noted, had undergone a wonderful transformation all of its own, and now it was even more magnificent than it had been before; broader, longer, its fat, purple head now atop a long, gleaming shaft which sported a thick, bulbous base.

And whilst Alyssa longed to stuff the thing all the way in her mouth 'till it stretched out her cheeks and pressed at the back of her throat whilst she sucked and gobbled upon it, Alyssa found that just the thought of that magnificent dick plunging inside her throbbing pussy made her entire body shudder with delicious pre-orgasm.

In the blink of an eye, Wolfram flipped Alyssa over onto her stomach; the rough pads of his huge paws scraped against the soft skin of her flanks, setting it alight - although he took great care not to cause her delicate skin harm with his sharp claws.

Alyssa squirmed beneath her lover, her breasts rubbing against the bear rug, her nipples hard and grinding pleasantly against the rough, sensuous fur. She raised up her hips to greet her lover, sensing that he was poised and ready with that glorious werewolf cock between her wide-spread thighs.

With a loud grunt, Wolfram thrust forward. His superlative cock slipped down between Alyssa's buttocks where it slid over the puckered hole of her ass and down into the soaking hot flesh of her pussy.

Alyssa let loose with an ear-splitting shriek; the all encompassing pleasure of having Wolfram's glorious cock filling her vagina for its very first time was almost too much for her to bear. She experienced every wonderful fraction of an inch as it parted her lips, stretched her sensitive entrance and plunged deep down inside her body, extending out the wrinkled walls of her hole almost to bursting. And Alyssa thought that for the first time of having a dick inside her pussy, this had been well worth waiting for.

Alyssa bucked her hips to meet Wolfram's increasingly intense thrusts, mesmerized by the touch of his coarse fur against her smooth skin and the ever so slightly softer touch of his underbelly that rubbed against her bare buttocks. She desperately wanted him as deep inside her as he could possibly go, to cram every single, solitary molecule of that hard, animal cock into her pussy, to slam its bulging head hard against her cervix.

Wolfram fucked Alyssa hard, his breathing a strained, breathy pant that felt hot and sweet against her sweetly perspiring back. He pulled out his cock almost to the point of leaving her raw, wet flesh, only to plunge it back in again – an action that elicited an orgasmic cry and a wild thrust of shapely hips from his lover.

Close to orgasm now, Alyssa could feel the pressure building in the deepest depths of her pussy, and she felt as if she was about to *literally* explode. Wolfram had lowered his weight onto her back and was fucking her like a wild, rutting animal, and with that and the enveloping touch of his rough fur, Wolfram drove Alyssa further towards climax.

"Bite me," Alyssa moaned, and lifted up her head. She turned it the best she could to look into his eyes. "I want to be like you," she said.

Without breaking his stride and with the fat meat of his cock buried to its bulging base inside Alyssa's pussy, Wolfram craned his lithe neck down towards the white skin of Alyssa's shoulder and nipped at it.

Alyssa gasped at the sharp stab of pain that ran all the way down her spine and she buried her face in the bear skin. She then felt a warm, wet trickle of blood run down her shoulder blade and with that she came.

"Oh, *fuck*!" Alyssa screamed, not caring if her voice carried over the entirety of the house. The orgasm exploded violently through her, sending wave upon wave of pleasure through her body. Every square inch of Alyssa's skin lit up in a vivid pink flush that glowed beneath the glistening sheen of her sex-sweat, and the very depths of her vagina felt as if they were on fire.

And still Wolfram thrust his cock deep and hard into her, stretching the flesh, pounding hard into her quivering body.

Alyssa felt herself begin to change.

It was a weird – and incredibly *pleasurable* – sensation that bubbled beneath the pulsing heat of her orgasm, prolonging the tsunami of pleasure that smashed through her senses. It felt to Alyssa as if things were physically *moving around* inside her body; bones and tissues and organs each taking up new positions.

The hair that sprouted over Alyssa's body was silky, smooth and luxurious - a direct contrast to Wolfram's rough fur that had rubbed her naked ass cheeks to a glowing red color. She could also see her own snout now, her nose black and glistening wet at the end of it, and her teeth felt alien in her mouth, as if they belonged to someone else.

Watching Alyssa's transformation as he fucked her had sharpened Wolfram's gratification to the extreme. Seeing his young lover as an animal akin to himself drove him inexorably towards his own climax, and he slammed hard against Alyssa's still transforming buttocks to push his cock roughly into her tightening pussy, knowing that when she came a second time, her newly rearranged muscles would clamp down hard on him, locking his cock inside her body until her animal ecstasy was over with.

The two grunted and yelped and growled as they fucked each other with frantic urgency on the bearskin rug, their sharp claws churning up the pelt, digging thick tufts out of it as their pleasures reached an inevitable crescendo.

Alyssa's body was still awash from her first orgasm, and her body remained alight from her transformation into a primal beast, her senses heightened to the extreme, and yet she felt her climax building yet again as Wolfram slid his cock in and out of her pussy, and his guttural sounds let her know that he was close to his own peak.

With a loud, shrieking yowl that echoed out across the forest, Wolfram came. He slammed his pelvis hard against Alyssa's body, driving his dick deep into her vagina as his ejaculate pulsed hard and fast from his body. Alyssa felt her werewolf lover's fluid pumping into her body like liquid fire, and she felt an aching, *pulling* motion deep in her gut that she imagined to be her cervix slurping up Wolfram's semen like some cheap, greedy dockside whore.

And that was the sensation that sent Alyssa screaming over the edge of her second orgasm – more violent and intense than before, now that she was complete in her new physical state - and she howled and bucked and felt the taut muscles of her vagina clamp shut around Wolfram's cock, trapping him inside her. And that sensation felt so incredibly breathtaking that Alyssa wanted to keep her lover inside of her beautiful beast's body forever.

A shape at the window.

Broad, tall, it filled the frame, all but blocking out the moonlight that had illuminated the torrid scene on the bearskin, the two werewolves locked together as one huge, bristling, panting monster.

In the blink of an eye, the figure leapt from the window ledge. It landed with preternatural grace on the stone floor of Wolfram's boudoir; its monstrously curved claws scratching deep grooves in the ancient slate. The creature rose up on thick, powerful hind legs, its pointed snout curled up in a snarl with cruel teeth glinting wickedly in the chilly, silvery light.

Reactions slowed by his post-coital fugue, Wolfram responded to this unexpected intrusion a heartbeat too slow. And in the time it took him to withdraw his penis from the tight confines of Alyssa's slippery wet pussy, the trespasser was upon him.

Alyssa howled out her protest as Wolfram's cock was pulled from her body, her vagina doing its very best to hold onto him. Inadvertently, she found that she relished the ripples of residual pleasure that coursed through her newly altered body, despite the obvious danger presented by the new arrival to their tryst. Alyssa lashed out with one paw to slash at the intruder's flank as he wrestled Wolfram off her and onto the cold stone floor. And when Alyssa righted herself, standing to face the intruder on all fours, her haunches taut and coiled like springs ready to leap, she saw that there were bloodied clumps of fur wedged between her claws.

Wolfram fought back with aplomb. Snarling, growling, his powerful jaws snapped at the throat of the assailant, his hind legs kicking hard at the vulnerable underbelly of the werewolf that had him pinned against the hard floor. Somehow, despite his attacker's advantageous size and superior strength, Wolfram managed to dislodge the beast and struggle upright.

From the safety of the space at the side of Wolfram's huge bed, Alyssa watched as Wolfram and his opponent circled one another, vicious teeth bared, claws flexing, golden flecked eyes glinting with menace as each werewolf awaited that split second of distraction that would allow a strike.

The door to the bedroom flung open, creaking loudly upon its ancient hinges like some grotesque, complaining creature. The Mistress hurried in, a cocked shotgun nestled in the crook of her arm, and a no-nonsense expression etched in her icy features.

"Sal," she growled.

And in that heartbeat's diversion her arrival provided, the intruder had launched himself full-force at Wolfram, knocking him clean off his feet.

Wolfram countered, digging his claws into the other werewolf's thick fur, fighting through the matted coat to slice at the soft flesh beneath, his fearsome canines snapping shut a mere hair's-breadth away from his attacker's throat.

But the intruder was too big and too strong for Wolfram, the obvious advantage of youth allowed him to overpower his victim and razor claws churned through Wolfram's dark pelt, turning it into a glistening wet mess. Valiantly, Wolfram fought back from the vicious onslaught, snarling, barking, clawing and struggling from beneath the sheer bulk of the other werewolf, his flanks dripping blood, his breath coming out in thick, labored, liquid gasps. Without hesitation, the moment he regained his feet, Wolfram launched himself once more at the intruder, gaping jaws and foaming teeth aimed with deadly accuracy at the other's exposed throat.

With an agility that belied his size, the interloping werewolf sidestepped Wolfram's attack. The older wolf's teeth clacked together mere inches from his throat, so hard that a fractured canine tooth flew high and glinting white into the air. And then the two were locked together again, back in their deadly embrace that looked for all the world to be some perverse parody of Wolfram and Alyssa's earlier fucking.

The Mistress hovered in the background, aiming the twin barrels of her weapon at the mêlée, unable to take a clear shot for fear of hitting her master.

Alyssa watched with mounting horror as her lover succumbed to the relentless onslaught of the mysterious werewolf, the creature that had so rudely interrupted her post-coital bliss and the feel of Wolfram's thick, long cock buried deep inside her body. She chomped her teeth together, relishing the feel of the long, curled canines as they ground against one another, and she stared down at the curved, keen claws that had sprouted from her once delicate hands.

She made a decision.

Wolfram flailed beneath the bulk of the other werewolf, his energy draining away with the copious amount of blood that his wounded body was leaking onto the floor, his growls and snarls now more of desperation than raw anger. His attacker clawed and bit and kicked at his prone body, drawing yet more blood, driving the very essence of life from him.

Alyssa sprang at the werewolf just as it lowered its mighty jaws down towards Wolfram's throat to deliver the final *coup de grace*. Although she can have weighed in at less than half the size of her lover's assailant, the element of surprise plus the momentum of Alyssa's jump knocked him off Wolfram, and sent him sprawling on to the thick pile of the rug that was still damp from Alyssa's sex-sweat.

Wolfram struggled back to all fours, his blood-soaked body struggling for breath. He turned to face his enemy, the glint of recognition sparking in his dulling eyes.

Taking her chance, the Mistress fired off a shot and the recoil of the shotgun all but knocked her off her feet. The shot hit the werewolf in a hind leg just as he leapt at Wolfram. The wolf yowled in pain and surprise and crashed clumsily into Wolfram, the pair of them colliding with the four-poster in a tangled mass of bloodied limbs and snarling, snapping jaws.

Alyssa sprang at the pair, aiming her sharp claws at the werewolf's shoulders, clamping her teeth down hard on his vulnerable nape. The wolf snapped and growled and bucked his body to try shake her off, but Alyssa held tight, her hind legs scrabbling frantically against the creature's back.

And yet, despite the brutal wound to his leg and Alyssa's assault on his back, the werewolf savaged Wolfram like he was nothing more to him than an errant and irritating puppy. Blood flowed, flesh tore and bones snapped as Wolfram howled with the white heat of the pain that ripped through his body, his life ebbing away with each drop of spilled blood.

The intruder heaved the massive bulk of his blood-soaked body, flexing the powerful muscles that throbbed like monstrous machines beneath his gore-matted fur. Alyssa was flung from his back like a troublesome insect. Flailing, her body crashed into the Mistress and the pair of them tumbled head over heels. The Mistress's head connected hard with the unforgiving stone floor with a resounding *clunk*. The twelve-gauge flew from her hands, firing off one last shot harmlessly into the crackling logs that sparked and jumped in the fireplace.

Alyssa's head swam, the sense knocked from her with the fall as sure as the air had been from her lungs. The sights and sounds of Wolfram's bedroom swam in and out of her awareness, until all she could her was her lover's laboured, rattling breaths and the *click-clack* of the interloper's sharp claws on the floor. Closer, closer still they came, until the huge, snarling muzzle of the werewolf was staring directly down at her and Alyssa could see the fine shreds of her lover's flesh sticking to the long, cruel teeth that were stained red with blood.

Powerless to fight, unable to do anything other than gaze up into the gaping maw of the werewolf, Alyssa felt her body shifting, changing. And as she slipped from her animal form, Alyssa became once more aware of her naked skin, her heaving, blood spattered breasts, her nipples that jutted angrily at the wolf, her lover's fluids leaking hot and thick from her pussy that was once again human. The werewolf raised one mighty paw and brought it down so quickly that it *whooshed* in the cool night air.

Then, all went very, very black for Alyssa Bowers.

Chapter Four

"There is no way on God's green Earth he will produce an heir now," one of the handsome young men said with a smug laugh. "All of this – the house, the land, the companies – is practically ours now." He grinned as he fondled the exposed breasts of a half-naked and incredibly nubile young woman who was perched obediently upon his lap. Playfully, he tweaked each of her cherry-red nipples in turn, delighted at the startled squeak his actions elicited from the black-haired girl.

"You talk as if the old man is already dead, Valentin," another of the half-dozen spoke up. "You would do well to remember that he is not."

"The families are optimistic, yet cautiously so, Pyotr," a third joined in, his voice labored as a girl with long, red tresses slurped noisily at his not insubstantial cock.

"It will only be a matter of time," another of the young men added from his place in the center of the huge bed that dominated the orgy room. "Which is why the families have asked us to remain here." He glanced nervously at the thick oak door that was firmly bolted closed, as if someone could possibly be listening in at their subterfuge. Of course, he had little to worry about, what with Brecht still in his coma following the attack, and the Mistress maintaining her round-the-clock vigil at his bedside like some sad, love struck schoolgirl.

"And that is such a chore," the first of the young men – a particularly beautiful and commanding individual by the name of Timur laughed once more. "We have to sit and wait, with very little to distract our – *appetites*." He jiggled the girl on his lap's bare breasts for emphasis, his gold-flecked eyes sparkling as mesmerized he watched them bounce and wobble.

"I say we make the best of a bad situation," Valentin said. "What say you, Maxim?"

But Maxim was in no position to add much to the conversation, his head buried as it was between the alabaster thighs of a buxom young wench who squirmed and sighed at the attentions of his busy tongue. He did, though, manage a muffled, wet *mmmmfffff* from the slippery depths of the gal's eager, wet pussy.

The sixth member of the nefarious group, a dark, brooding young man named Yakou, sat quietly at the far side of the room, his tanned, naked body framed perfectly by the tall-backed mahogany chair he'd claimed as his own. Silently, his fingers laced and steepled beneath his chin, his long, fat erection jutting out from his lap like some altogether alien creature, he just listened and *watched*.

"I think it's time for you to earn your supper," Valentin said to the girl who wriggled upon his lap. His hand slid up her skirt and between her milky thighs. "I think my friends and I would appreciate a little entertainment now." He pulled his hand out from the girl's skirt, his fingers glistening wet from her vagina. He slipped them into the girl's mouth and she suckled upon them greedily. Once Valentin's fingers were cleansed of her sweet, piscine taste, the girl slid from his lap and sashayed over to the huge bed, skilfully discarding her white cotton skirt as she went. Valentin eyed the dark haired girl's beautifully pear-shaped ass which swayed hypnotically as she walked. "I find that town whores are far superior to the village whores, wouldn't you agree, Max?"

Maxim emerged from between his whore's thighs, sending her on her way over to the bed with a loud slap on her bare ass. He grinned at the reddening outline of his hand that appeared on the milk-white skin. "I actually like the village prostitutes," he said, "they are more accommodating and somewhat cheaper in price." He smiled across at Bogdan who was struggling to remove the red head from his dick. "But then again, with the town girls, no one seems to miss them."

"Watch your mouth, Max," Timur barked. "If Brecht ever heard you say that – "

"Brecht is in no position to hear anything we say," Pyotr chimed in as he clambered from the bed to give over the vast expanse of white cotton sheets to the dark haired girl and the pale skinned beauty. "Which is just as well for us, I guess," said with a nervous smile and another glance towards the door. "And even if he were, our leader is certainly in no fit state to do anything about it."

The red head finally extricated herself from Bogdan's immense erection and made her way over to the bed, her delectably bare feet slapping gently against the stone floor. "Which means that we are free to do whatever pleases us," he added to the conversation with an air of finality.

And in the short space of time that it took the red headed girl to reach the bed and climb onto it, the other two girls had already begun their performance.

The six young men turned their attention to the three naked town girls who knelt upon the bed. The pale skinned, large breasted girl – a natural blonde, as was made evident by the wisps of fair downy fluff on her plump, pouting pussy lips – kissed the dark haired girl full on the mouth, her tongue sliding between her gently parted lips, eagerly seeking out its playmate. Briefly they wrestled tongues, licking, lapping and tasting one another, each drinking down the other's warm saliva like it was nectar from the heavens. The dark haired girl caressed her lover's firm, bountiful breasts, raking gently across the white skin of each tit with her long, manicured nails to leave red, glowing track marks. She then took each nipple between fingers and thumbs and tweaked at them, ever harder than before, until the blonde girl groaned out her pleasure softly into her plaything's mouth.

The red head took her place next to the two, her hands stroking their naked buttocks, fingers dipping into both curvaceous cracks to explore warm, moist, intimate places. She pushed her head towards the others' and joined in their kiss; three hot, wet pairs of full lips joined together, three eager, slippery tongues caressing, tasting, six hands stroking, scratching, kneading, exploring.

Timur and his fellow hedonists – with the notable exception of the all-too-quiet Yakou –

approached the bed, eyes wide and sparkling, eager to be close to the show the young ladies were putting on for them.

The red head and the dark haired girl lay the blonde down on the crisp, white sheets, her firm and unblemished body aglow in the shimmering moonlight that snuck through the windows. And in an instant, she had the dark haired girl suckling at her breasts like an esurient infant at its mother's teat and Redhead nuzzling between her parted thighs, inquisitively seeking the warmth there with her flicking tongue. The blonde girl arched her back, threw back her head and closed her eyes, her pale skin flushing a luxuriant pink as pleasure washed through her. She moaned and bit down hard upon her lower lip as she succumbed to the meticulous attentions of her sapphic lovers.

The redhead gently pushed at the blonde's legs, urging the silk-smooth thighs wider apart to expose the deliciously dark pink flesh that lay between them. She nudged at the tiny, jutting bud of the girl's clit with the tip of her nose, whilst at the same time brushing her tongue around the slick entrance to the other girl's vagina. In synchronicity, the dark haired girl sucked hard upon the blonde's left breast, drawing the entirety of the broad, stiff nipple – along with a goodly amount of quivering tit – into her mouth, her tongue massaging it with languorous, hard movements whilst her hand massaged the blonde's right breast with firm, kneading strokes.

Redhead ventured a finger into the sodden hole between the blonde's engorged, glistening pussy lips, first parting the delicate inner labia so that her pussy resembled an exotic – and especially beautiful – butterfly. Pleased at the moan this action elicited from her muse, Red slipped a second – a third – finger inside the tight vagina, crooking them to better massage the blonde's g-spot.

The blonde girl writhed and moaned softly as her pussy was stretched wide by the trio of busy fingers, her hips bucking gently to welcome them all deep inside her hot, wet hole.

The dark haired girl licked her way down from the blonde's breasts, leaving a glistening trail along her sternum, down to the sensuous indent of her navel, all the way until she was wriggling her tongue alongside the red head's upon the swollen nub of the blonde's clitoris.

The blonde girl cried out in ecstasy as two lithe, busy tongues lapped at her clit, driving her ever onward towards the inevitability of orgasm. She buried her hands in her lovers' hair, grabbing red hair and black by the fistful and driving both girls' faces hard onto her sex.

The redhead broke the sensual circle first, pulling her head away from the damp, musky scent of the blonde's wet pussy, her face made deliciously slick by her lover's juices. The blonde moaned out her disappointment at this, as if having one tongue lapping at her sensitive spot simply wasn't enough. She moaned even louder when the red head's fingers slipped from her vagina and left her slippery wet, pouting and decidedly *empty*.

As if under some unspoken direction, the dark haired girl also pulled away from licking at the delicious pussy, her lips shimmering with sweet, sticky juices. She knelt up and took a hold of one of the blonde's legs, holding it apart from the other and aloft.

Timor, Valentin and the others (again, with the notable exception of Yakou, the group's consummate yet distant voyeur) shuffled closer still to the bed until their thighs were pressed hard against the mattress. Their erections stood firm, proud, moistened with glistening pre-cum and pointing eagerly at the trio of beauties who were by now so deeply engrossed on one another's firm, young bodies.

So much so, that not one of the young women noticed the subtle changes in the men; a slight elongation of the jaw lines, a rapidly spreading sprinkle of coarse body hair, a lengthening of dark finger nails.

As the six men looked on, each and every one of them all but physically drooling, the red head slipped a long, shapely leg beneath the blonde's and positioned herself so that her sopping pussy was aimed directly at the blonde's. She eased downwards, taking support from the blonde's legs that were held firm by the dark haired girl, until her pussy caressed the blonde's slick labia and it looked as if the two slippery wet pussies were engaged in a long, passionate kiss.

The blonde moaned deeply, her eyes closed tight, her body flushed. She raised up her hips to meet the red head's, pressing her hot wetness hard against the pussy that had been so wonderfully presented to her. She rocked her pelvis in time to the red head's slow, rhythmic movements, grinding her clit against her lover's, squeezing their engorged and incredibly slick pussy lips together.

The dark haired girl held the blonde's leg tight against her ample bosom, pressing her nipples tight against the muscular calf. She bent down her head and flicked her tongue across the line of delicate, sexy toes before popping a couple in her mouth to suck upon them.

This drove the blonde into a sexual frenzy. She bucked and ground and writhed against the red head's pussy, determined to gain her salacious pleasures from the girl's firm, wet heat as their juices mingled and bubbled out from between them.

As the young girls scissored, the loud, orgasmic cries of the redhead and the blonde filling the room, the men climbed on to the bed – even Yakou who had finally vacated his seat across the room. The six men, their features transforming into something altogether less human, slunk across the crisp white sheets, their attentions fully focussed upon the naked, cavorting ménage.

Redhead came first. Long, hard and loud. She ground her sopping pussy hard into the blonde's, rocking her hips with deep, powerful movements, her clit squashed against the blonde's clit as she masturbated herself on her lover.

"Fuck, fuck fuck!" the blonde yowled out her climax, her hands squeezing at her own breasts as a master baker kneads his precious dough. She tugged hard upon her fiercely jutting nipples, the pain she brought forth from the sensitive flesh serving only to further heighten her pleasures. She bucked her hips upwards as high as she could, almost lifting the red head from the bed, determined to prolong the orgasm that had set her senses so astonishingly alight.

And, as the blonde and the redhead came, and the dark haired girl held tight onto the smooth, pale skinned leg of her lover as she suckled upon her dainty toes, the six men – now more beasts than human beings – were upon them.

At first the six did nothing more than lick at the three girls; tasting, drinking, and savoring the slick sheen of sex-sweat that adorned each one of their young, nubile bodies. The girls giggled and moaned, the extra attention adding more pleasure to the heady glow of their orgasms. And then the men-beasts began to nip at the soft vulnerable flesh, and the three girls' giggles quickly turned into cries.

Once the first drop of blood was drawn – by Pyotr who nipped hard at the dark haired girl's breast, sheering off the stiff nipple that topped it – the werewolves descended upon the three sapphic lovers in a vicious feeding frenzy.

The redheaded girl barely had time to scream. She extricated herself from the blonde, her pussy shiny wet from the both of them, and attempted to shuffle away. Valentin and Bogdan prevented her escape, their long, curved claws digging cruelly into the soft flesh of her flanks to pull her back into the affray, whilst with one swift snap at her vulnerable throat, Maxim silenced her forever.

Timor, Yakou and Pyotr snapped and ripped and tore at the naked flesh of the other two girls, their pelts matted by the powerful arcs of the red head's arterial blood, their long snouts buried deep inside the girls' bodies, seeking out the sweetest, most succulent flesh that lay hidden within.

The merciful release of death came quickly to the three young girls, and their bodies – skin still flushed with the afterglow of their climaxes – were devoured greedily by the werewolves. And then, no sounds save the shredding of skin, rending of flesh and snapping of bones could be heard in the room as the six beasts consumed their feast.

Chapter Five

Brecht Wolfram stirred in his bed, his hair matted upon the sweat-soaked pillow. He groaned out loud and shifted his wounded body, catching his breath in his parched throat as pain radiated out from what felt to be every nerve ending he possessed.

"Welcome back, Master Brecht," the Mistress greeted him with a smile. She leaned forward in the faded leather armchair that stood by the bed and clasped his hand with both of hers.

Wolfram gave her the best smile he could manage, although it pained his ravaged face to do so. "It is good to see you," he said, his voice a hoarse croak. "I thought you were – "

"My wounds were nothing," the Mistress dismissed his concern with a wave of one hand. "I healed quickly."

"How long?" Wolfram asked. His brow furrowed as he recalled just how badly the Mistress had been hurt during the fight.

"There is no need to concern yourself with that right now; you must concentrate on getting well again."

"*How long?*" Wolfram growled and gripped the Mistress's hand – so tight that the bones crackled and shifted.

"Seven weeks," the Mistress replied and her grimace gave away the discomfort in her hand.

Wolfram's grip relaxed and he sighed, long and loud, the air rattling in his dry windpipe. "And Alyssa?"

The Mistress shook her head, no words necessary.

"The bastard took her," Wolfram said, tears brimming in his eyes. "My foolish brother's idea of revenge for Anichka, no doubt."

The Mistress said nothing. She reached over to the nightstand and plucked a small, brass bell from its ornate mahogany stand. She jingled the bell, its high pitch carrying through the room like the shrill tone of an exotic bird. In an instant, the bedroom door opened and a young girl entered. She carried a white enamel tray upon which sat a glass and a large jug of iced water, fat, irregular chunks of ice jingling melodically within.

Wolfram eyed the girl as she walked across the room. Her eyes flicked nervously to and fro, as if searching the room for something. Her high, firm breasts bulged from the tight top of the simple, white cotton dress that clung to her voluptuous curves like a second skin, her own skin silky smooth and startlingly flawless. Wolfram's eyes shifted from the barefoot girl's body and over to the Mistress, his question clear yet unspoken.

"She is new," the Mistress told him, "from the village."

Wolfram smiled a greeting at the girl as she placed the tray with great care upon the night stand next to his bed. She poured out a glass of cool, crystal water and a handful of ice cubes clinked loudly as they tumbled from the spout of the jug. "Thank you," Wolfram said as he took the glass from the girl's trembling hand. He took a long, deep drink, relishing the soothing coldness of the liquid on his arid throat – it felt to him as if he had not tasted water in an eternity.

"And what of the business?" Wolfram turned once again to the Mistress. The young girl backed up a respectful distance away from his bed; there, she remained in her spot, as if awaiting dismissal. "Am I to assume that the Families have been taking care of things?"

The Mistress' face told Wolfram all he needed to know. Of course, he was not to know about how the six Family representatives had insinuated themselves not only into his home but into his companies as well. Nor did he know about how they sated their cruel appetites with girls brought in ostensibly as maids and cooks. But, from the nervous twitch of the Mistress's eyes, Wolfram knew right then and there that *something* was terribly amiss. And yet, business be damned, his only thoughts were of Alyssa and the passion they had shared; the unrestrained, uninhibited *fucking* – and of the fact that he had given in to her request and had bitten her without so much as a second thought.

"You need to build up your strength," the Mistress broke the silence between them. "Before you can even begin to think about doing anything about your company, or the girl."

"I must find her," Wolfram said. He paused to slurp at the glass of water once more, this time draining it in one go – ice and all. "If she is with Sal, then she is in terrible danger." He placed the glass back on the tray. "I must –" Wolfram tried to sit up, but his body advised otherwise, sending sharp jolts of pain the length of his spine to put him firmly back in his place.

"And you will," the Mistress placated. "But all in good time, Master Brecht. You are no use to man nor beast in this condition." She attempted a smile that unfortunately came off looking a tad pitying. "Although I can see that not all of you is incapacitated." She glanced down at the all too conspicuous bulge in the bed sheets where Wolfram's erection had tented the high thread count Egyptian cotton. It would appear that the strength of her Master's magnificent erection was above that of the rest of his broken body, even though he was in mourning for his surrogate-cum-lover. And so, the Mistress slipped a hand beneath the sheets, seeking out the warm hardness that lurked there.

"There really is no need –" Wolfram began his protest. He was stopped short by the touch of the Mistress's cool fingers as they wrapped firmly one by one around his aching shaft.

The Mistress glanced across at the serving girl who had brought in Wolfram's water, and who remained steadfast in her place. And upon that silent cue, the girl lifted up her dress to reveal her naked pussy which was sweetly adorned with a dark triangle of fuzzy black hair. The girl slipped a hand between her thighs – slightly parting them as she did so – and gently pulled apart her pussy lips with long, wriggling fingers. With her inner pink flesh so exposed, the girl sought out the tiny bulge of her clit with her forefinger. Making certain to maintain eye contact with Wolfram, the girl began to masturbate for him.

Wolfram's already turgid cock stiffened yet more at the sight of the young girl's perfectly smooth, pale skin and shiny wet pussy – her finger busy at its swollen nub, her juices bubbling from her slick cleft and trickling down the insides of her thighs. And all the while, the Mistress kept up her slow, steady strokes at his dick, massaging it towards a much-needed climax.

As the orgasm built up inside Wolfram's battered body, throbbing deep inside his aching prostate and cum-heavy balls, he could feel his body beginning to thrum with an inner energy, the unmistakable energy of the ferocious beast that dwelled within him. As the Mistress masturbated him – and the young girl fingered her sopping pussy for his visual pleasure - almost imperceptibly Wolfram's jaw line altered and his teeth lengthened in their sockets. His body hair sprouted up along his back, which gave Wolfram a maddening itching sensation – he wanted nothing more than to scratch at it with his extending fingernails but that amount of strength eluded him for now.

The young girl continued to finger her pussy, pumping in and out of the tight, wet hole with two fingers, her thumb planted firmly upon her clit, her face flushed dark pink with pleasure. She moaned sweetly between gently parted lips, her nipples hard and dark against the flimsy material of her virginal dress, the liquid flesh of her tits jiggling with her exertions.

Wolfram cried out when he came, his raw throat making a sound more akin to the howl of his inner beast than that of a man in the throes of ecstasy. His body stiffened despite the pain that flowed through it, and he pumped spurt after spurt of hot, sticky fluid over the Mistress's hand and into the bed sheets.

The young girl squealed out her own orgasm. She gripped tightly at her pussy, her fingers embedded in the hot, slick flesh, the pad of her thumb crushing her clitoris hard against her body as if to squeeze out every last iota of the climax she had conjured for the delectation of her master. Her body shuddered and she froze, immobilized by the waves of pleasure that pounded through her young, nubile body, her alabaster skin aglow with the sensual dark pinks of sex.

Wolfram let out a mighty sigh. He slumped back into his damp pillow, his aching body tingling with the machinations of the healing process – accelerated by the Mistress's administrations to his cock. He watched as she pulled her hand from beneath the already cooling, sticky sheets and proceeded to lick his cum from her fingers – one by one, as meticulously as one would after a particularly tasty meal. His eyes told her *thank you* and as she slurped down his fluids and the young girl hastily rearranged her dress with slippery wet fingers, Wolfram fell into a deep and troubled sleep.

Chapter Six

Alyssa awoke slowly, her brain taking its own sweet time in waking up. At first, the crisp, green-hued light streaming through the curtainless window hurt her eyes as she attempted to get them to open to greet the morning, but after a moment or two, the harsh sting of the early morning daylight dissipated.

She rolled over in her bed – the bed in the locked room *he* kept her in at night, her waking brain reminded – enjoying the feel of the cool part of the sheets against her naked body.

Although she had all but lost track of time since she'd been brought against her will to this place somewhere in the depths of the forest, Alyssa had seen a full moon come and go, and through the rare cloudless sky the previous night, she had seen that the moon was well on its way to another. She had grown to welcome the fullness of the moon, since that was when she would transform into the magnificent beast that Wolfram had made her -

although she had discovered recently that she was able to affect that change *without* the benefit of the moon, albeit in a clumsy and only partial way. Alyssa had promised herself that she would practice everyday until she could achieve a full metamorphosis in broad daylight, during a waning moon. Until then, she was careful to conceal her attempts; Alyssa wanted to keep it to herself until the opportunity to escape arose, although she would indulge herself a little late at night, changing her body just a little whilst she fingered her aching pussy and rubbed frantically at her clit.

Of course, Alyssa had no idea where she was. Not only was she in the darkest depths of some foreign, unpronounceable land, she had been entirely unconscious (and totally naked!) during her transportation – all she knew for certain was that there was a vast sea of tall, majestic pines all around the modest cabin that she considered her prison – albeit a cosy, homely one – and that she was at a higher altitude than at Wolfram's mansion. She had no idea who the guy was who had brought her to this strange, gilded cage – the man who had been the werewolf the Mistress had called Sal – nor why he had done so; but what she *did* know was that he was as particularly untalkative as he was outstandingly attractive, and that he clearly had absolutely no intention of letting her go.

The girl who brought Alyssa her food and fresh clothes – a pretty young thing named Darya – offered some relief of human contact, although her accent was almost impenetrable and her English poor. She did however have the most delightful, petite body with firm, perky breasts and often Alyssa would find herself fantasising about undressing Darya, laying her out on the big, comfortable bed and lapping at her pussy until she made the girl cum. And, although Alyssa had not acted upon her carnal thoughts, she would often make sure that she was naked when Darya brought in her breakfast.

Alyssa's shoulder had healed quickly. The bite that Wolfram had administered at her insistence itched maddingly the closer the days came to the full moon, so much so that Alyssa longed to be able to will her claws to grow so that she could scratch at it – all the way down to the bone if necessary. In fact, the only time the itching had left her completely alone was when she was fully transformed.

There came a knock on the door, a gentle, almost hesitant knock.

"Yeah?" Alyssa grunted. She kicked the bed sheets down to the foot of the bed. Then she stretched out to enjoy the warm caress of the morning's light upon her bare skin.

"I have your breakfast," Darya's soft, sweet voice filtered through the thick wooden door.

"I'm awake, you can come in," Alyssa called out. It was somewhat amusing to Alyssa that the young girl always knocked since she was in effect one of Alyssa's gaolers *and* the door was kept locked at all times.

Alyssa listened to the sound of the key turning in the lock. She glanced over as Darya made her way into the room, balancing the breakfast tray in one hand and Alyssa's clothes in the other. Alyssa made no attempt to hide her nakedness from the girl. Instead, she sat up in the bed to afford Darya an unhindered look at her full, firm breasts in all their glory. She smiled. "Good morning, Darya," Alyssa said.

"Good morning," Darya replied, a coy twinkle playing in her deep, dark brown eyes. "I trust that you slept well."

"I did, thank you." Alyssa eyed the door that Darya had left half open.

"That is good," Darya said with a warm smile. She, too glanced at the door, but made no attempts to go back to close it.

Alyssa sighed and puffed out her chest, her nipples noticeably stiffening in the warming sunlight that glowed on her body. She knew – Darya knew – that even if she were to seize the opportunity and run, there would be little point; just where the hell was she supposed to run to?

Darya placed the tray on the bottom of the bed, resting it close to Alyssa's bare feet with a sneaky glance up at the dark tuft of hair that peeked out from between Alyssa's thighs. The tray contained a stack of wholegrain toast, a selection of cold meats of indeterminable origin, and a pint glass of milk. At the sight of the meats, so artistically arranged upon a simple, silver platter, Alyssa began to salivate. She watched closely as Darya laid out her clothes on the bed – a simple cotton dress that Alyssa knew would cling tight to her body (they all did!), matching panties and what appeared to be a pair of sturdy, knee-high riding boots.

"Salamao has asked if you would care to join him on the hunt this morning?" Darya said, although it did appear to Alyssa to be more of a demand than a polite request.

Alyssa studied the girl, trying to read her face, but instead found her eyes wandering over her long, silky black hair that cascaded all the way down to Darya's shapely ass, and the dark crack of cleavage that was displayed to perfection by the girl's low-cut dress. "That sounds – *interesting*," Alyssa ventured. "And why would I go hunting with someone I don't know?" She plucked a handful of meat from the platter and nibbled on it.

"You know his name, and you know his home," Darya replied, genuinely puzzled. "What else is there to know?"

"Aside from *who* he is, and *why* he brought me here, I can't think of anything," Alyssa attempted a smile.

Darya clearly didn't grasp the nuances of sarcasm. She furrowed her brow, which somehow made her stunning features all the more beautiful, and stared at Alyssa. "Salamao will tell you what you need to know all in good time," she offered. "Perhaps this is why he has invited you to go hunting today?" The girl appeared pleased with this explanation. She smiled at Alyssa, her eyes hungry and exploring Alyssa's naked body from nipples to toes.

Alyssa squeezed her thighs together, delighting in the serving girl's scrutiny, enjoying the tingling sensation that the increased pressure on her clitoris elicited. She leaned forward to pluck more meat from the silver plate, her breasts jiggling slightly as she moved.

"Unless there is anything else, I shall leave you to your breakfast," Darya said. "If you could be dressed and ready in an hour, please." She turned, back towards the door.

"There is one thing, Darya," Alyssa surprised herself, having never felt quite so brazen.

"Yes?" Darya turned to face Alyssa once more.

"I would like a little help with this," Alyssa purred. As she spoke she stretched her legs apart, giving Darya a perfect view of the already wet flesh between her smooth thighs. She rubbed at a nipple with her fingers, tweaking the puckered skin there to a firm, jutting point.

"I – er- I don't know –" Darya's voice faltered, her accent thickening. Yet for all her reticence, she couldn't help but stare at the pink, glistening folds of Alyssa's pussy that winked out at her from the sparse tangle of pubic hair.

"Close the door." Alyssa instructed, once more surprising herself. "And lose the dress."

Darya did as she was asked, and in the blink of an eye was standing naked by the side of Alyssa's bed, her own nipples erect and angry red atop her perky teacup breasts. With one hand she covered her pudendum, although the thicket of pitch black, curly hair that sprouted there peeked around her slim fingers.

"There's no need to be shy," Alyssa reassured, "I have wanted to taste you for a long time now."

At this, Darya took a step or two backwards, a hint of fear on her pretty face. Her free arm jumped up to cover her breasts, as if offering them some modicum of protection.

"Oh, I'm *so* sorry," Alyssa said with a sheepish smile. "I didn't mean it like *that*." She made a mental note that in future she really was going to have to keep in mind her new state of being – especially if she was not going to terrify her potential conquests. Having said that, there was an underlying curiosity inherent in Alyssa now as to just how Darya's young, firm flesh would actually *taste*, how her blood would feel trickling down Alyssa's throat as her life was snuffed out. Alyssa shook her head as if to chase those thoughts away. She had a much stronger – and far more urgent – itch to scratch. "Come," she said softly to the girl, patting a space on the bed next to her bare thigh. "Join me."

Somewhat hesitantly, Darya clambered onto the bed, her modest breasts swaying, her inner pussy lips pouting out through her luxuriant pubic hair. She manoeuvered herself so that her head was facing Alyssa's pussy, her long, silken hair draping down over her shoulders to caress the smooth, sun kissed skin of Alyssa's bare belly

"What are you waiting for?" Alyssa said, her voice hoarse with lust. "Eat me out, Darya."

Ever obedient, Darya lowered her soft, sweet lips down onto Alyssa's pussy, her tongue darting out to taste the slick juices that moistened the fleshy slit. The tip of it nudged against the bulging head of Alyssa's clit. Alyssa jumped as an electric wave coursed up through her body to make her flesh tingle and glow all the way up to her stiff nipples. Unable to resist any further, Alyssa gripped Darya's hips and shifted the girl up over her head, so that the girl's delicious pussy was positioned directly over her face.

With a sigh and a deep inhalation to savor the scrumptious, musky perfume of Darya's sex, Alyssa coaxed the girl's hips downwards – until the plump dampness of Darya's labia were pressed against her lips. She flicked her tongue the full length of the moist cleft, delighted that Darya tasted every bit as good as she had imagined – the wonderful salty-sweet flavor of youth and fresh, pink flesh. Alyssa sighed against Darya's pussy lips, as she felt the girl's tongue part her own labia and wriggle downwards towards the slippery wet entrance to her vagina. Alyssa lifted her hips slightly to press her clit against Darya's chin, moaning softly at the pleasure that radiated out from her sensitive nub.

Darya lapped at Alyssa's pussy, eager to please, happy to be pleasuring the pussy she had so often admired. She dipped a finger into the slick hole, curling it upwards to massage the faint lump of Alyssa's G-spot, all the while having her tongue dance light-but-firm around the swollen head of her lover's clit.

Alyssa gasped as Darya's finger penetrated her aroused entrance. She groaned out loud, her voice muffled as she pressed her face harder onto Darya's pussy, her busy tongue slipping into the taut hole that nestled within. She gripped the girl's tight, muscular buttocks to pull their bodies together until she could barely breathe. The full length of Darya's body now lay atop Alyssa, the two girl's skin alight where it touched, their perspiration mingling and their beings almost as one.

Darya worked with vigilance at Alyssa's pussy, slipping another finger deep inside the tight walls and stretching the powerful muscle of her vagina, all the while rubbing with strong, deliberate strokes at the wrinkled insides of her lover. With her mind on her own pleasure, Darya gently ground her own swollen, sensitive sex against Alyssa's face, working towards her own climax that she could feel bubbling up inside her.

"Oh!" Alyssa cried out, her voice suppressed against the wetness of Darya's intimate flesh. "Oh, *fuck*!" She felt her body begin to give way to the orgasm that Darya had so expertly created, her skin afire, senses swirling.

Darya, too, released her pleasures; her own climax thundered through her tiny frame to make her body shudder from head to toe. She couldn't help but thrust her hips hard against Alyssa's slippery wet face, her actions entirely involuntary.

Alyssa fucked the girl's sweet pussy with her mouth, matching each thrust of Darya's hips with a counter jab of her long, strong tongue and the tastes poured out from the girl, igniting Alyssa's senses and stirring the now all too familiar beast within her. Alyssa felt the sensation of her teeth stretching in their sockets, the delicate bones of her face shifting, her finger nails beginning to grow. Then she came a second time, this orgasm even more powerful than the first. Her muscles clamped down hard on Darya's fingers, so much so that Alyssa actually *felt* the poor girl's knuckles pop inside of her own vagina Alyssa yowled out her climax and grasped Darya's firm ass cheeks, her extending nails digging into the soft, smooth, sweat-dampened flesh.

"Ow!" Darya cried out and her fingers slipped from Alyssa's sodden, squeezing pussy. She pulled her head away from between Alyssa's thighs, her face dripping wet with clear, slick juices, the moment gone.

"I am *so* sorry," Alyssa panted, struggling to regain her breath in the fierce afterglow of her monumental and much-needed orgasm, her threatened transformation quickly receding. Shamefully, she glanced down at Darya's buttocks as the girl clambered from the bed. There, Alyssa saw ten tiny crescents, each one oozing a miniscule crimson droplet of blood. "I really didn't mean to-"

"It's okay," Darya said with a placatory smile, the hint of fear sparking in her eyes. "It happens."

It was then that Alyssa saw the myriad tiny white scars that peppered Darya's buttocks, and all the way up the graceful curve of her back to her sleek shoulder blades. Alyssa sat there on the bed in the dampness of her own perspiration, her face sticky wet with Darya's pussy juice, and couldn't help but wonder just what the girl had experienced in her short life, and just what exactly her relationship with the mysterious Salamao was.

Darya dressed quickly. She ran shaking hands through her long mane of hair in an attempt to get it back into some form of order. She then smiled at Alyssa, her lips glossy, her face still flushed from the afterglow of climax and the gentle abrasiveness of Alyssa's sparse pubic hair. "I must go now," Darya said - at once back to her detached persona. "And don't forget, you are to be ready in one hour." She took a long, lingering glance at Alyssa's wonderfully naked body, as if committing to memory every delicious inch of the girl, and then took her leave.

*

Alyssa stepped out into the morning sunlight, its tree-filtered beams reflecting off the white dress that she had been given to wear. It was the same dress – or at least the same style – that she had worn from the first day here, and she often puzzled as to whether it was the same couple of dresses worn and washed in rotation, or if Sal had a whole warehouse full of the things. The crisp, white cotton of the dress clung to Alyssa's curves and accentuated her breasts. It was scooped at the front – although not improperly so – and its hem fell about her knees. Today, of course, she had on the riding boots, the leather of which was so incredibly soft that they felt as if she had worn them for years. This was a novelty for Alyssa since she had been barefoot for the entirety of her incarceration, which suited her just fine since the furthest she had ever ventured was to the soft, verdant grass that surrounded the cabin. To have ventured into the forest would have meant braving the brambles and thorns and jagged sticks that littered the floor beneath the towering trees in her bare feet – and Alyssa guessed that was most likely the point.

"You look good, those boots suit you," Sal called over to her. Alyssa turned to face the man, shielding her eyes as she did so from the harshness of the sun. He sat astride a huge gray mare and urged it to trot towards Alyssa with gentle nudges of his knees against its flanks. He brought the horse to a stop by Alyssa's side, its snorting breath hot on the cool, bare skin of her décolletage.

"Thank you," Alyssa – polite to a fault – could really think of nothing else to say. She stared up at Sal like some star-struck teenager, taken aback at just how damned hot he looked all stripped to the waist with mighty thighs bulging as they gripped the heaving flanks of the horse – the two appeared almost as one magnificent beast.

"Thank you for joining me," Sal said with a genuine smile. "I was hoping that you would."

Alyssa looked up at Sal's tanned, handsome features, his unruly mop of black hair, majestically curved Roman nose and gold flecked eyes that were so dark brown as to appear practically black. She forced a smile; they were both fully aware that she had absolutely no choice in accompanying him on his hunt, her only question was *why* he had given her the invitation.

"Come," Sal offered Alyssa his hand, his broad palm and long, powerful fingers extended out towards her. Alyssa took it and Sal lifted her up onto the horse as if she weighed nothing at all. Alyssa gasped as she found herself sitting so high up – the horse was taller even than it had appeared from the ground. The saddle was smooth, well-worn brown leather, and it slipped between Alyssa's legs like an old, familiar lover. The dress rode up to expose the full length of her smooth, white thighs to the world, and Alyssa was pleased that she had decided to put on the panties – white cotton of course – that had been so thoughtfully left for her by Darya.

Sal urged the horse on, and as the animal began to move Alyssa had no option but to throw her arms around the man's waist, discovering that his hard, muscular body was so broad that she could barely reach all the way around him.

And so, with her sun-warmed, supple body pressed tight against that of her half naked captor, her senses tingling from his proximity, Alyssa was taken deep into the emerald darkness of the forest.

Chapter Seven

The six young men stood around Wolfram's bed with an odd mix of eager anticipation and disappointment on their faces; they put Wolfram in mind of a motley flock of starving buzzards that were somewhat disheartened to find that their planned dinner was feeling decidedly better. They had brought along with them an attractive threesome of beautiful young ladies, none of whom Wolfram recognized. Each one of the dark haired beauties was more buxom, more attractive than the next. Wolfram had the impression that the six had brought the girls along for the express purpose of tormenting him, clearly underestimating his rapid healing process.

"It is good to see you in such good health, Brecht," Timur lied with a sincere smile. "The Families were concerned about you."

"I am fine," Wolfram said. "I am growing stronger with each passing day. I will be out of this bed by the next full moon." He smiled and made eye contact with each and every one of them, relishing their obvious unease.

"In the meantime, you can rest assured that the businesses are all being well taken care of," Bogdan threw in.

"You could take longer with your recuperation, if you needed to," Pyotr added with a shifty look in his eyes. Wolfram had never trusted that one; he always seemed to him to have a hidden agenda - with *everything*. In fact, the only one of the six Wolfram mistrusted more was Yakou - that young man hardly ever spoke a word, he just seemed to forever hover in the background and *observe*.

"Thank you for the kind offer, Bogdan," Wolfram replied. "But I think I have already spent far too long on my sick bed, don't you?"

Again, the collective unease spread across the six, much as even a stifled yawn passes from person to person. Wolfram knew full well that the six wished him dead. Had Salamao finished him off on the night that he took Alyssa away, through them the Families would have gained total control over the Tungsten Industries empire and everything that went along with that. For in the absence of an heir, that was the way of the werewolf's global community. But now, now that Wolfram was well on his way to making a complete recovery – and along with that the chance to sire that elusive heir – the six, and the Families were in effect back on the bench.

"It will be good to have you back at the helm," Valentin managed at least a modicum of sincerity. "The Families have missed you." He whispered something into one of the girls' ears and in unison the three pulled open their shirts and stepped forward towards Wolfram's bed.

"For you, Brecht," Maxim said. "Take one, take all three if you have the energy." He cracked a wicked grin, his eyes dancing gaily over the three pairs of magnificently bare breasts.

"The Master has no strength for such frivolities!" the Mistress barked at them all as she entered the room. Ignoring the look of obvious disappointment on Wolfram's face as he eyed each of the buxom maidens up and down with a hungry glint in his sparkling eyes, she shooed the girls away from the bed. "You must conserve your energy for healing," she admonished Wolfram as she might an errant child. "I think it is time for you all to leave now," she said to the six, and made sweeping motions with her arms to emphasis her words.

Timur ushered his five cohorts from Wolfram's boudoir, along with the three dark haired girls. He cast a backwards glance at Wolfram with a hateful look in his eyes.

"They really ought to know better," the Mistress fussed as the door closed behind Timur. "Anyone would think they didn't want you to get well." At this, she tipped Wolfram a sly wink. As the Master's eyes and ears in the mansion, nothing happened without the Mistress knowing about it, although she had chosen not to tell Wolfram about the fate of the previous batches of servant girls – had she done so, she knew that he would have forced himself from his bed before his body was fully healed. Instead, she had kept that particular piece of information quiet, placating herself with the knowledge that such things were constantly inherent in Wolfram and his kind, and that once

Wolfram was back fully in control, things would change. "You must rest now," she plumped Wolfram's pillow to settle him down, her lips pursed.

"Thank you for saving me," Wolfram's sarcasm wasn't lost on the Mistress. "Those girls looked absolutely terrifying." He laughed and noted that whilst the Mistress's mouth turned up at the corners, there was an indiscernible hint of *something* in her eyes.

Jealousy?

"Sleep," the Mistress urged. "The quicker you heal the better."

"You are right, of course," Wolfram acquiesced as he settled his huge frame back against the crisp, cool sheets. "I have my brother to find – and Alyssa."

And there was that look on the Mistress's face again.

*

The pulsing heat from the horse's body, along with the bumping motion the creature made as it pushed on through the forest was working minor wonders on Alyssa's clitoris. With each movement, a tiny jolt shot up through her pussy and made her bare thighs tingle deliciously where she tightly gripped the animal's flanks. It also helped that she was pressed up so close against Sal's naked back, his body hot and gently perspiring, her arms snaked tightly around his muscular waist.

They'd been trekking into the forest for what had seemed to be hours, the foliage and undergrowth growing ever thicker and filtering out yet more of the sun's warming light until it seemed to Alyssa that twilight had crept up on them ahead of schedule; its hue a rich green, its air chilled. Still, the more than pleasant sensations that the horse's movements were generating down in Alyssa's pussy were more than compensation for that, as was the rich, earthy scent that seeped from Sal's pores, a faintly animal bouquet that hinted at the beast that dwelled just below the surface of his taut, flawless skin.

"Almost there," Sal told her, his voice deep yet quiet. Alyssa *felt* his words rather than heard them – other than the soft clucks of his tongue to encourage the horse ever onwards, they'd been the first thing he'd uttered in an age.

Alyssa looked around. This part of the forest looked to her to be pretty much identical to the part they had just come through, *and* the part that stretched out before them. Just how Sal knew where they were was beyond her. She had also realized – some miles back – that Sal didn't appear to have brought along any weapons for his hunt, not even so much as a bow and arrow. And for the first time since he'd snatched her from Wolfram's mansion, Alyssa felt genuinely afraid of the man; what if she were to be the quarry in this particular hunt?

At once they happened upon a clearing. It was as sudden and unexpected as the bright shafts of sunlight that penetrated the forest canopy to light up the ground in a startling display of golden-green. A host of insects – gaily patterned butterflies, dragonflies and a multitude of buzzing, darting things that no doubt feasted upon blood - cavorted in the warmth of the sun's light, their activities interrupted only by the small birds that swooped down amongst them to fill their beaks and bellies.

"Here," Sal grunted. He slid from the horse's back and offered up his arms to Alyssa, his hands resting on her sweetly sweating thigh.

Alyssa took Sal's huge, strong hands and allowed him to pluck her from the horse and lower her gently down to the spongy, moss-covered ground. Alyssa was disappointed to be away from the wonderfully stimulating motion if the horse, of the animal's raw, animal heat that had stoked the lustful fires within her loins. She could feel that her sex was deliciously damp in the warmth of her panties, her pussy radiating out its aching, wanton heat all through her body. She looked up at Sal's huge frame that towered masterfully above her; at the broad, sweat-slicked chest, the bulging musculature that rippled beneath his tanned skin, and at that moment Alyssa wanted nothing more than to have her vagina crammed full of his long, thick cock.

She ventured her hand over Sal's sharply defined six-pack, her fingers tracing the outline of the solid muscle there, taking delight in watching his flesh twitch beneath her touch. Alyssa's hand crept downwards, and she noted that Sal's breathing had become a shade deeper.

Sal looked down at Alyssa, the gold in his deep, brown eyes sparking in the sunlight. He cupped her face in his huge hands and leaned down to press his lips hard against her upturned mouth.

Alyssa flicked her tongue between his lips the instant they locked onto hers. She sought out the hot, wetness of Sal's tongue, the two slipping over one another, tasting and caressing. Alyssa tugged at the rough leather belt that encircled Sal's jeans, the strong smell of horse on him wafting up to her nose to heighten the arousal that grew with urgency deep down in the pit of her belly. Undoing the belt with trembling fingers, Alyssa tugged down Sal's pants to reveal a long, thick cock that was of an extraordinarily fearsome size even though it was still only half-erect. Alyssa grasped the hot shaft, pushing her hand downwards to peel back the taut foreskin and bare the bulbous purple head of Sal's throbbing dick.

In Alyssa's mouth, Sal's tongue increased its intensity, flicking and probing, sliding to and fro as he mouth-fucked her with it. Alyssa reciprocated, jabbing at his tongue with hers, wriggling past its onslaught to venture deep into the heat of his mouth.

Sal's broad, rough hands grasped at Alyssa's heaving breasts, kneading them with a hard urgency over the thin cotton of her dress. She ached to peel away the dress, to expose her bare skin to the warmth of the sun, to be entirely naked in the presence of Sal – her lover, her *kidnapper*.

Alyssa was just about to drop to her knees and take Sal's monstrous cock – now fully erect and pulsing like some untameable wild animal in her hand – into her mouth when there came the sound of something moving through the forest; crashing through the undergrowth with purposeful speed.

Sal pulled away from Alyssa and froze, his senses alert as his intense eyes studied the darkness of the forest.

Alyssa too stood rooted to her spot, all thoughts of that magnificent cock forgotten, although her pussy continued to soak her white cotton panties through.

A huge bear crashed through the forest and into the clearing, its thick, brown fur bristling in the dancing light, the creature's presence scattering all but a stubborn few of the darting insects. It studied Alyssa, Sal and the terrified horse with dark, malevolent eyes, it's dripping snout sniffing at the air, teeth bared in a vicious, hungry grin. Then it rose up on its hind legs, taller by its head and shoulders than Sal, its eyes burning into the humans that had dared venture into its territory.

Alyssa wanted nothing more than to run and just keep on running. But she knew that she would have little chance against the bear; she had it figured that the thing would have run her down and be snacking upon her entrails before she'd even managed to reached the edge of the clearing.

Sal took one step forward, towards the bear. His deflating erection remained quite formidable, its fat, purple head pointing towards the furious creature as if in some bizarre, silent threat.

The bear dropped back onto all fours, the look on its face now almost quizzical as Sal continued to move towards it, kicking his pants away from his feet as he did so.

The bear gave out an ear-splitting roar and charged towards Sal, its huge paws beating a heavy tattoo on the forest floor as they kicked up a flurry of dead leaves, its massive bulk rippling in the light, vast jaws agape and filled with monstrous, glinting teeth.

Alyssa gasped and shrank back behind the horse; although the sick knot in the pit of her belly told her that the poor animal would offer little protection against the vicious teeth and claws of the bear, should the beast make it that far.

In the short space of time that it took the bear to cross the clearing, Sal had transformed into his other self - the huge, ink-black werewolf. Without hesitation, he launched himself at the bear, letting out a piercing howl of his own.

The bear hesitated just a little.

It was to be a hesitation that would lead to the poor creature's undoing, for Sal was upon the beast before it could regain its composure, his mighty jaws clamped hard around its neck. The bear roared out in pain and swiped at the werewolf that clung on to its back, claws digging into the thick fur for purchase. The two crashed to the floor, fallen branches snapping about them like dry kindling, molding leaves and clumps of bright green moss kicked up by long, vicious, scrabbling claws.

Alyssa watched, rapt, as the beast that Sal had so effortlessly morphed into wrestled with the bear, his thick pelt absorbing the blows from the animal's massive paws, his teeth chomping at the thing's nape.

And then, in an instant, the bear turned the tables. It shook Sal from its back, and his jaws snapped shut on nothing more than thin air. The bear then rolled over and pinned Sal to the ground, the bulk of the werewolf's body pressed hard into the forest floor beneath its weight, his powerful hind legs trapped beneath the bear and quite useless. Unable to stand and watch any longer, Alyssa took a long, deep breath, pulled her dress up over her head and kicked off her boots. Then, clad only in her flimsy panties, Alyssa charged towards the bear, hoping to all that was holy that she had mastered the whole transformation thing at least enough to pull off this daring manoeuver.

Alyssa's body changed with remarkable speed as she sped across the forest clearing; no doubt the quickness of her metamorphosis into the wolf-state was accelerated by the vast amounts of adrenaline that coursed through her system. She felt the soft cotton of her panties rip apart as her hips contorted and her thighs became wider, and she dropped down to all fours without so much as breaking her stride.

In what seemed to have been no more than a half dozen heartbeats, Alyssa had covered the distance between herself and Sal, and launched her fully-transformed self at the huge bulk of the bear that had her kidnapper pinned to the ground, its huge, salivating jaws snapping at his throat. Alyssa's weight was no match for the bear's, but still she managed to catch the beast by surprise; it had been so intent upon forcing its fierce teeth through Sal's powerful forelegs to tear out his throat that the sudden appearance of the she-wolf on its back caused the bear to drop its guard for just a split second.

And in that moment, as the bear twisted its head around to greet its new attacker with a guttural roar, Sal had his long, narrow jaws clamped firmly around its vulnerable throat. And with a violent shake of the werewolf's head, there came the unmistakable sound of rending flesh and the bear's angry voice was cut off mid-roar.

Alyssa was flung from the creature's back and her body landed with a loud *thump* on the forest floor, the breath knocked from her lungs. The bear rolled off of Sal's body, its attention taken now by the hot, spurting jets of blood that pulsed from the ragged hole in its throat. It wheezed and coughed up thick gobbets of scarlet blood as it rolled its huge bulk around, painting the soft, verdant grass a sickly crimson. Both Sal and Alyssa were caught in the gruesome rain created by the bear's death throes, their fur drenched with sticky blood, their noses filled with the cloying, coppery scent of spilled blood.

Finally, the bear lay still, its huge body limp and lifeless with blood oozing lazily out of the gaping wound in its throat that Sal had made. Alyssa trotted over to where Sal lay, her body making its transformation back into something more human. Sal, too began to change, and as his pelt retracted back into his body, Alyssa could see the thick, purple bruising that ran the full length of his left-hand side, and the deep scratches the bear had made across his belly – had Sal been without the protection of his werewolf pelt, the beast would have surely eviscerated him. Already Sal's wounds were beginning to heal, and Alyssa was surprised to find that she was actually *relieved* that he was alright.

Alyssa was back to being entirely human – and completely naked – by the time she got to Sal. Her body was drenched with the bear's blood, it felt hot and slippery on her skin, a feeling that she was somewhat nonplussed to discover made her feel incredibly horny. It also appeared to have had a similar effect upon Sal, his blood spattered, naked body sported a most impressive erection which he made no attempt to hide.

And in that moment, Alyssa discovered that she had never wanted someone as much as she did Sal right then and there.

"That was a stupid thing to do, you could have been killed," Sal said to Alyssa. He sat up and smiled, his bloodied face slick with sweat. "Thank you." He reached out to stroke Alyssa's cheek, his eyes glancing down at her naked breasts, dallying awhile over the hard, jutting points of her nipples.

"I couldn't help myself," Alyssa replied. She rested a hand upon Sal's thigh, ignoring his wince as she brushed against the vivid, purple bruise that blossomed there. "I couldn't really have stood by and watched as that thing ripped you apart."

"It would have been your chance to escape."

"And ride around lost in the forest by myself?" Alyssa laughed. "Just how long do you think I'd have lasted?"

"But still-"

"And just maybe I didn't *want* to escape." Alyssa slid her hand upwards, until her fingers were resting against Sal's formidable erection. "Maybe I like you all in one piece and breathing." She leaned towards Sal and pressed her lips against his, her tongue parting his lips to invade the soft warmth of his mouth. She curled her fingers around his rock hard cock and molded her bloodied, sticky body into his.

Sal let out a sigh at the delicate touch of Alyssa's fingers. Involuntarily, he bucked his hips upwards, gently fucking her hand. He met her probing tongue with his and tasted the hint of blood that had snuck into her mouth, the tart, metallic tang serving to further stoke his arousal.

Alyssa clambered on top of Sal, her pussy dripping wet and aching to be crammed full to bursting with his long, broad cock, her animal desires overriding every emotion that she knew she ought to be feeling towards the man who had abducted her from Wolfram's mansion and who had kept her prisoner – albeit in a most picturesque gaol.

She slipped the hot hardness of Sal's prick between her slightly parted pussy lips, holding it there, caressing it with her slick flesh. Rocking her hips, Alyssa gently massaged him, wetting his erection through whilst at the same time stimulating the tip of her throbbing clit. And then, slowly, teasingly and without breaking their passionate kiss, Alyssa manoeuvered her tight entrance over the pulsing, bulbous tip of Sal's cock.

"They have killed the bear!" a voice boomed across the clearing, cruelly breaking the moment.

"Praise be to our guardians!" another joined in.

Alyssa froze, her slick hole mere inches away from Sal's glorious prick.

Then, she watched as a dozen or so rugged looking men stomped into the clearing, crashing through the undergrowth with even less grace than the bear. Between her thighs, Alyssa felt Sal's cock deflate a tad, and her own lascivious thoughts of fucking him whilst covered in the blood of their kill dissipated like an early morning mist.

"We shall declare today a holiday and hold a feast in their honor!" an elderly man said rather grandly, and Alyssa couldn't help but wonder if she'd somehow slipped into a 1950's vampire movie.

Alyssa climbed off Sal and helped his battered and bruised body up from the forest floor. She brushed away the dead leaves that had stuck to his back with the flat of her hand. She then faced the villagers who still approached, seemingly not at all concerned that the two bear killers were stark naked and covered with sticky bear blood. Alyssa tried her best to cover her breasts and pussy with her hands as the men drew close, but still she felt incredibly vulnerable.

Sal, on the other hand, stood there with his hands on his hips, his semi-flaccid penis still a magnificent specimen, his big, broad chest puffed out with pride and the bear's blood drying on his skin in the sun's warming light.

"We owe you so much," one of the men said, ignoring Sal's blatant nakedness to shake his hand. "That bear took my daughter, and three of the village elders," he explained with sadness in his eyes. "I am pleased that it is dead."

"It shall make a handsome feast," the elderly man spoke up, and Alyssa saw that drool had formed at the corners of his mouth. "You will be our guests of honor?" Unashamedly he eyed Alyssa's nude body up and down with an appreciative smile on his face.

"We would be honored," Sal replied. He slipped a sideways glance at Alyssa, the golden specks in his eyes twinkling mischievously.

"That would be nice," Alyssa told the old man, somewhat reticent at the thought of eating bear meat, even though she understood it to be quite scrumptious.

"Then it is settled!" a portly, middle-aged man at the back of the group declared. "We shall prepare the village's finest virgins!"

"The what now?" Alyssa whispered to Sal as they surreptitiously made their way back towards the horse – and their clothes.

"Just go with it, accept their gratitude in all of its forms." Sal grinned at her.

Alyssa shrugged, figuring that she had little choice in the matter and that she really ought to make the most of whatever the overly grateful villagers had in store for her by means of a celebration. Having said that, Alyssa really hoped that she wouldn't be expected to eat any of the village virgins - that really would be one step too far, even for the werewolf part of her.

Forlornly, Alyssa glanced down at her panties that lay crumpled in a tiny heap on the ground; they were pretty much ripped up beyond all recognition. She sighed – riding Sal's horse *sans* underwear really wasn't going to do much to help the unfulfilled ache that throbbed deep down inside her pussy.

Chapter Eight

The village was not quite the primitive log cabins and mud huts that Alyssa had in mind. It was certainly small, little more than a single main street with a handful of stores and five or six offshoot streets that were adorned with randomly spaced white boarded, two-storey houses. At one end of the unimaginatively named Main Street, and adjacent to the church, there spanned a spacious village green which was home to an impressively sized barbeque pit.

It was upon that very pit that the villagers roasted the hastily prepared bear carcass – the creature had been skinned and filleted with lightning speed and now huge slabs of its bloody meat were duly skewered and being turned slowly on the numerous iron spits that sat over the roasting coals. The bulk of the animal had been mounted upon a huge wooden stake and placed on the largest of the spits directly over the center of the pit. Alyssa watched the high, yellow flames dancing, and inhaled deeply the delicious, aromatic perfume of the roasting meat. She guessed that the people of this particular village in the middle of the forest were somewhat accustomed to eating bears.

They'd mounted the poor creature's head on a tall, wooden pole and placed it at the outskirts of the village as a warning to others who may decide to partake of a tasty villager or two – but just how effective that would prove to be was anybody's guess. So far, all Alyssa could tell was that the severed head was particularly efficient at attracting swarms of shiny, black, fat-bodied flies.

Alyssa and Sal had been taken into separate homes to clean up, washing the dried bear blood from their bodies to emerge an hour or so later looking like something more human. They'd also been presented with fresh clothes, and Alyssa was especially pleased to be wearing panties once more – the thought alone of the bumpy trip back to Sal's cabin on the back of his mare made Alyssa's vagina throb – she'd all but climaxed twice earlier on the short trip from the clearing to the village.

As evening fell, and the village's children were all safely tucked up in their beds, the festivities began.

A huge bonfire was lit in the center of the green, its flickering yellow flames shooting high up into the cloudless sky that was already littered with a speckling of bright, twinkling stars. The village band played lively folk music for the people to dance to and fat chunks of bear meat were passed around along with succulent cobs of sweetcorn and crusty honeycombed bread that melted in the mouth.

Alyssa and Sal were, as promised, the guests of honor. They had pride of place at each end of the long table the villagers had laid out and which literally sagged at its center beneath the weight of all of the food. And whilst Sal lapped up the attention – particularly that of the seemingly countless parade of nubile young maidens who fussed and fawned over him – Alyssa couldn't help but feel more than a little awkward. After all, she really hadn't done much more than distract the dumb bear; it wasn't as if she'd killed the thing with her bare hands or anything. And besides which, she had some unfinished business with Sal and that magnificent cock of his – her moist pussy lips still tingled at the memory of its hot hardness pressed against them. And as she looked across the distance of the table at Sal laughing merrily along with the hot young women, his eyes roaming across the exposed cleavages and gravity-defying bosoms, Alyssa couldn't help but feel a little bit jealous.

Once most had eaten their fill of the tender bear meat, the music stopped. The villagers had Alyssa and Sal stand shoulder to shoulder before the gathering. The village elder – the old man who had lead the group which had so rudely interrupted Alyssa's planned fuck in the forest clearing before it had even gotten started – clapped his hands together to command everyone's attention. A reverent silence spread across the gathered villagers; all that could be heard was the crackling of the fire and the faint cries of the creatures of the forest.

"Once again we give thanks to our guardian and saviour," the old man declared in a grand voice. "And to his mate." He swept an arm in Alyssa's direction. "They have saved countless lives with their ungodly powers, as the Wolfram family has done throughout the generations."

A cheer rang out, followed by hearty applause.

"Now that we have fed their bellies, we must feed their souls, as tradition dictates."

Alyssa looked across at Sal. He returned the glance and offered a lascivious upturn of his lips.

"Bring forth the virgins!" the old man raised his voice.

Alyssa looked nervously around, picturing in her mind a gaggle of nubile young women skinned and skewered in much the same way as the bear. Her stomach churned, for as much as she'd enjoyed the sweet, gamey bear meat – its rare-cooked flesh flavor had definitely piqued her new-found tastes - she really didn't think that she could face eating people meat right now; even if she was to change into her werewolf state.

From within the church there came a group of young men and women. They filed out in pairs – a guy and a girl – six pairs in all. And each and every one of them was entirely naked.

Sal eyed the approaching group with hungry eyes, appraising each of the young ladies' firm, smooth-skinned bodies as they sashayed towards him and Alyssa.

Alyssa couldn't help but ogle the young men – and a couple of the gals caught her roaming eye too, with their high, firm tits, puffy pink nipples and sparse smattering of fair pubic hair – relieved that she obviously wasn't expected to consume any of them, and delighted to see that large cocks were apparently a thing in this particular village.

The dozen young, naked villagers stopped directly in front of Sal and Alyssa. They fanned out – boy, girl, boy, girl – in a line so that their guests of honor could see each and every one of them in all of their naked glory.

"Pick one," Sal whispered to Alyssa.

"Pardon me?" Alyssa whispered back, butterflies tickling her stomach.

"We are expected to pick one each, unless there isn't a virgin here that takes your fancy?" Again with the salacious smile.

"But-" Alyssa started.

"Just pick one, Alyssa," Sal reiterated. "You mustn't offend these people." He spoke slowly, his lips barely moving as he scanned the line of nubile young bodies. The girls all returned his gaze with nervous smiles, their hands by their sides and admirable chests puffed out to offer up an uninhibited view of their innocent young bodies.

Sal stepped forward and held out a hand to a flaxen haired girl at the very end of the line. Taking his cue, Alyssa also stepped forward and picked the guy standing next to that girl.

"Good choice," Sal whispered, "they are together." He winked at Alyssa, studying the young couple's faces as they exchanged nervous glances.

A murmur of approval spread across the crowd as they parted to allow the remaining ten virgins to return to the church. Sal and Alyssa watched them go, taking in the sheer beauty of their firm, shapely buttocks as they made their way away from the gathering. And Alyssa was certain that there was a definite air of disappointment amongst those five couples.

"What now?" Alyssa asked Sal. She had 'her' guy by the hand, an action that had led to an instantaneous hardening of his long, thick cock.

"We fuck them of course," Sal replied. He had his arm draped around the blonde girl's beautifully white shoulders, one hand cupping a generously sized breast.

"Where?"

"Here."

"Are you serious?" Alyssa studied the crowd, all of whom had adopted an air of eager anticipation.

"Do you want to offend the whole village?" Sal sighed.

"Of course not, but-"

"Then you must do what is expected," Sal told her. He removed his arm from the girl's shoulder and quickly undressed, his erection standing proud as a clear indication of his approval of the village's selection.

Once more taking Sal's lead, and feeling more than just a touch self-conscious, Alyssa stripped off the clothes the villagers had so generously provided earlier in the day. And when she stepped out of her panties and shoes, standing there as naked as the day she was born, her tits and pussy displayed for all to see, Alyssa felt an electric tingle run all the way up from her clit to her fiercely jutting nipples.

Sal lay the girl down by the fire, gently lowering her petite body onto the soft, flattened grass. Her hair fanned out behind her head, glowing iridescent in the light of the flames. She parted her legs to allow Sal access to her most intimate part, her pussy lips parting to allow him entry. She glanced downwards, between the twin mounds of her pert breasts, her eyes wide with wonder at the massive cock that was aimed directly at her slick entrance. She gripped Sal's biceps as he mounted her, clearly unsure as to what she was expected to do.

Alyssa lay down besides the girl, their bodies almost touching. She beckoned the young man towards her, lifting her knees and parting her legs to guide him. He knelt down between Alyssa's feet, his cock twitching and shiny wet with pre-cum, his eyes swimming with lust at the sight of her exposed pussy. Alyssa took hold of the guy's arms and pulled him on top of her warm body, relishing the touch of his skin on hers. She wriggled beneath him, manoeuvring her tight hole towards the bulging tip of his cock, letting it rest there awhile, delighting in the look of sheer disbelief on the young man's face.

Sal had waited for her. And now, seeing that Alyssa was poised, he slid his thick, meaty cock inside the blonde girl's vagina, bending his head to suckle her left nipple deep into his mouth. The girl let out a loud groan and bucked her hips upwards to meet his first thrust, driving his dick deep inside her tightness.

Alyssa followed the young girl's lead and lifted up her hips. This had the effect of slipping the young guy's cock between her engorged lips and into the awaiting heat of her vagina. She gasped as the young man's girth stretched her tight walls and pulled teasingly on the hood of her clit. She ground her hips against his, encouraging him to begin thrusting – determined to finish what Sal had started back in the forest.

The crowd cheered at this – their offerings duly penetrated, tradition appeased. They stepped back – just one step – to allow the copulating couples a soupcon more space, but continued their voyeurism.

Beside Alyssa, the young blonde girl moaned, her lithe body undulating beneath Sal's bulk. She threw out a hand, finding Alyssa's. She held it tight, her moans already reaching their inevitable crescendo.

Perhaps it was seeing his girlfriend in the throes of orgasm, or maybe it was that he was experiencing the tight heat of a real life pussy for the very first time in his life, the young man fucking Alyssa began to thrust wildly into her with the unmistakable fervor on one who is about to climax. Alyssa tried to clamp his pelvis with her thighs, but to no avail; his body was coated with a slick sheen of sweat, his skin too slippery for her to exert any form of control over his movements. And as she watched, the guy's face contorted and flushed bright red. He grunted and snorted like a wild animal trapped in a snare, and Alyssa felt his cock pulsing and jerking deep inside her body as he pumped spurt upon spurt of hot, sticky cum into her.

The blonde girl squealed loudly as she came, her hips crashing hard against Sal's, her hand crushing Alyssa's as orgasm swept through her sweet, tight body. Her pretty young face scrunched up in much the same way as her young man's and Sal pulled out of her pussy, experience telling him that she was now far to sensitive down there for him to carry on to his own completion.

The crowd cheered again.

Although the ritual had not lasted long, they all seemed happy with the result; their offering of two young innocents to the guardians of their village had once more been a resounding success.

Sal smiled at the crowd as he got to his feet and helped the girl up from the floor. He planted a chaste kiss on her lips and hugged her, his cock still angry and fully erect.

Alyssa stood next to him, smiling her gratitude at the villagers as her young stud made his way back to his girl, his spent dick already drooping and his cum oozing out between Alyssa's labia to dampen her inner thighs. The young man took the blonde girl in his arms and led her back towards the church, away from Sal, Alyssa and the satisfied crowd.

Unlike the villagers, Alyssa felt far from satisfied.

She had been only just getting started on her orgasm when the young man had shot his load inside of her, and that had left her entirely unsatisfied and her body demanding release. What she really wanted to do – *needed* to do – was to finger at her aching clit until she found the relief her body so desperately craved, but something inside her psyche just simply wouldn't allow her to frig herself off in front of an entire village - despite them having just watched her being fucked. A sideways glance at Sal's thick, purple-headed cock told Alyssa that he too had been left spectacularly unfulfilled by the hot blonde. As sexy and tight as she had been, there clearly was no substitute for experience. And, although she had little experience of her own, Alyssa had the young blonde beat by a couple of fucks and one hell of a lot of anal sex.

So, Alyssa gave in to her animal craving, allowing her deepest carnal desires to take the lead. Brazenly, she took Sal's long, thick cock in her hand, delighted to feel that it was still slippery wet from the girl he had just fucked.

Sal moaned softly as Alyssa led him by his fiercely hard cock closer to the crackling fire and urged him down onto the soft cushion of the grass. He looked up at Alyssa, as if seeing her for the very first time, and there was something other than pure animal lust burning in his dark brown eyes.

Alyssa knelt beside him, his cock grasped in her hand, her breasts rising and falling with each deep breath she took. She paid no heed to the villagers who crowded around her, all eager for the entertainment to start up again, as disappointed as she and Sal at the brevity of the earlier couplings. She leaned over, her tits brushing against Sal's thick, muscular thigh, her nipples rubbing sensuously on the smooth, hot skin. She lowered her mouth down onto Sal's cock, inhaling deeply to savor its perfume – his hot masculine musk mingled with the sweet scent of virgin pussy.

He tasted even better than he smelled.

Alyssa slipped her mouth around the fat, bulging head of Sal's formidable member, caressing its tip with her tongue, probing into the slick slit at its end. She could taste him – of course – along with the subtle, salt-sweet essence of the young girl; a heady cocktail indeed. Beneath her, Sal groaned out his pleasure and gently rocked his hips to fuck her mouth. Deeper, deeper still, Alyssa allowed that wonderful cock to slide over her tongue until it was nudging at the rear of her throat.

The villagers looked on, rapt as Sal's dick disappeared inch by fabulous inch into Alyssa's mouth, and already some of them were undressing, openly masturbating or playing with others amongst the crowd.

Alyssa really couldn't have cared less if the entire village were fucking each other around her, for her entire focus was on Sal and his thick, meaty cock that stretched her lips wide as it slid ever so gently down her throat. Sal buried his huge hands in

Alyssa's hair, urging her onwards until her face was pressed against his pubic mound, his cock deep inside her mouth, the unmistakable shape of its bulbous meatus pressing out in her throat. He bucked his hips to throat fuck Alyssa; each thrust a little more urgent than the last, yet taking great care not to choke her.

There was an audible gasp from the villagers when Alyssa slid the entire length of Sal's mighty prick from her mouth. It bounced upright from his body, its head and shaft glistening wet in the firelight, steaming with its own heat in the cooling air of the night.

Alyssa looked around, at the villagers who were having a party of their own; young and old, couples, threesomes, moresomes – kissing, fondling, undressing. There were naked breasts, naked pussies and protruding erections in varying degrees of arousal everywhere Alyssa cared to look, yet eyes were still upon her and Sal, as if they were providing the necessary erotic inspiration for the burgeoning orgy.

Sal sat up, his face flushed, his cock achingly hard. He coaxed Alyssa down onto the warm, flat grass and positioned himself over her reclining body. Pausing, supported by his powerful, bulging arms, Sal contemplated the naked young woman beneath him. He sniffed the air around her, fucked every inch of her exposed skin with his eyes – from the sensual hollow at the base of her throat, to the firm mounds of her full breasts, down to the dark dimple of her navel, and yet further to the gentle bulge of her mound. There, Sal's cock pointed towards the slick slit between her thighs, making its intentions perfectly clear.

Alyssa stared up at the man on top of her, longing to feel the weight of his broad, powerfully built body pressing down on her, desperate to have him inside her – stretching, pushing, *filling*. And much to her surprise, she felt something altogether more subtle lurking behind the raw animal lust in her breast, something akin to *feelings* for the man-beast who was poised to mount her like she was a bitch on heat.

In perfect synchronicity, Sal thrust downwards as Alyssa raised her hips. The two locked together in an instant, Sal's cock sliding with slippery ease between Alyssa's swollen, parted pussy lips until its broad base was grinding against the tiny pink head of her clitoris.

The villagers *ooohed* and *ahhed* in unison, almost as if they were watching a spectacular fireworks display and not a couple fucking by a fire on the village green. Yet more of the people undressed, some of them now turning their attention to those around them; lips seeking lips, fingers groping for hard dicks and wet pussies, breasts being caressed and sucked.

Sal and Alyssa fucked each other. Slowly, sensuously, relishing every thrust along with each re-penetration as Sal's cock stretched Alyssa's tight entrance to its limit and filled her to capacity inside. She felt the fat, rubbery head of her lover bumping hard against her cervix, which in turn radiated out deep waves of pleasure that made her extremities tingle and throb. And, as Sal's pace quickened, Alyssa matched him, bucking her slim hips up to meet his, working hard towards her own explosive orgasm.

As he fucked Alyssa with those long, powerful, deliberate strokes, Sal began to transform.

This delighted the villagers to a point of frenzy, fuelling their sex party still further. Most of them were entirely naked now – even the elders who paraded their ancient flesh with pride, not caring a hoot who saw their low hanging breasts, drooping cocks or sparse, silver white pubic hair. Many were by now laying down and copulating in time to Sal and Alyssa's fucking, men atop women, women riding men, daisy chains of writhing, licking and fucking young couples, women frantically fingering women – there was even a trio of beefy young guys frottering their wide, glistening cocks together with expressions of sheer bliss on their faces.

Alyssa sensed the less than subtle change of Sal's cock inside her vagina. It broadened still further, pressing hard against her hot wet walls, the girth of its shaft easily as wide now as her own wrist. Where soft, smooth skin had caressed her belly and thighs, luxuriant hair sprouted and rubbed against her, its texture silky-soft with an underlying coarseness that heightened her arousal to an almost unbearable height. Alyssa watched as the bones behind Sal's face shifted, rearranging his handsome features into the lupine snout that she had first seen on that fateful night when it had been Brett Wolfram's dick that had crammed her to capacity and filled her with hot and creamy seed.

Without breaking his intensifying rhythm, Sal completed his transformation, and the beast he had become drove his monstrous cock hard into Alyssa's body. His fur rubbed against her flushed, naked skin, triggering every one of her nerve endings, driving her further towards an inevitable climax. Sal lowered his huge head and nuzzled at the soft mounds of her jiggling breasts, gently nibbling at each hard, cherry-red nipple in turn with his long, curved canine teeth, growling softly as Alyssa took hold of his long, pointed ears to urge him closer to her panting, perspiring body.

"Fuck me harder," Alyssa urged. "Make me cum, Salamao."

Sal thrust hard into Alyssa's vagina, pumping his cock deep inside the heat of her body, slamming hard against the swollen head of her clitoris. And beneath him, Alyssa's writhing and counter-thrusting increased to match his, her delectably firm buttocks bouncing off the spongy grass.

Alyssa screamed out her orgasm as unimaginable pleasure blasted through her body. Letting go of her beast-lover's ears, she grasped his heaving flanks, her fingers vanishing within the thick fur of his pelt. And still he pumped away at her body, for the moment lost deep within himself, every fragment of his being focussed on his own release. Alyssa cried out again and again, her cries and squeals turning to shrill howls as she transformed under the influence of the orgasms that just kept on racing through her shifting, changing body.

Finally, Sal came.

His entire body shuddered, his back arched and his jaws spread wide with an ear-splitting howl. With hard, involuntary stabs, Sal's cock pulsed and jerked as it emptied inside Alyssa's tight vagina, much of the resulting ejaculate oozing out of her along the length of his broad shaft. Beneath him, Alyssa had become a she-wolf, her fur caressing his, her claws digging into his flanks, her metamorphosed body even more arousing to Sal's werewolf state than her human form.

With one final yowl into the black, star speckled night, Sal pulled out from Alyssa, his cock sticky with cum and steaming with the erotic heat from their combined sex.

Around them, the villagers cavorted, all too wrapped up in their own orgy of sucking, fucking, sodomy and sexual experimentation to notice – or care – that the two werewolves had slunk away into the night.

Alyssa followed Sal into the darkness of the deep forest, in her animal form no longer afraid of what unpleasant and deadly things the densely packed trees may be harboring. She glanced back at the village green, at the undulating sea of naked, fornicating villagers that glistened and moaned in the dying light of the embers – the orgy would last until the first rays of the morning sun warmed the people's exhausted, spent bodies.

Bounding after Sal, eager to be close to him, Alyssa delighted in the sensation of his hot sticky fluid deep inside of her. And as they walked, the newly welcoming, lightless expanse of the forest swallowed them both up.

Chapter Nine

Wolfram called out for the Mistress from his bed. His body ached, but in a good way – it was the deep-down, dull throb of healing. His bones had mended a while ago, his flesh repaired itself, and now his scars were receding like footprints in wet sand. Such was the gift bestowed upon him and his kind; what made them ethereal creatures of the night had made them virtually indestructible.

"What is it, Master Brecht?" the Mistress bustled into the room, her hair in disarray, her clothing uncharacteristically askew. Wolfram smiled, no doubt the Mistress had been taking her pleasure from either one of the Six, or the stable boy. It was odd how it surprised him that beneath the icy exterior and eagerness to serve his every whim, the Mistress had her own salacious desires that required sating from time to time.

"Bring me one of the girls I saw yesterday," he said, "the one with the short hair will do just nicely." He gave the Mistress a lascivious grin. "I am feeling much stronger today." He glanced down at the all too evident tent in the bed clothes.

"I'm very pleased to hear that," the Mistress replied, straightening the rumpled hem of her dress that had ridden up her shapely bare thigh. "But I'm afraid that those three particular girls are no longer with us."

"They were new." Wolfram looked at her, puzzled. "Did they not enjoy working here?"

"I have no idea about that," the Mistress told him. "They spent the evening with Timur and the others and this morning they were gone."

At this, Wolfram appeared most concerned. He ran a hand through the rough stubble that sprouted on his chin, deep in thought.

"I can have one brought up from the village for you?" the Mistress, ever helpful, suggested.

"Thank you, no." Wolfram gave her a pleasant smile. "I think there are more urgent matters to attend to." He wriggled from beneath the bed sheets, not in the least bit bashful at exposing his thick, hard cock to the Mistress; it was not as if she'd not seen the thing before, after all. "I fear that the Six have been up to their nefarious tricks in my extended – and *enforced* - absence," he said as he reached for his clothes. "And if that is the case, they will also be plotting against me – the Families have had their eye on my empire for a long, long time."

"But-" the Mistress began her protest.

"But nothing, Mistress," Wolfram interrupted, pulling his pants up over his still jutting penis and taking great care not to catch the sensitive skin of its bulging head in the zipper. "I have spent far too long in this bed; I have healed enough to do what should have been done months ago."

"You are going to find her?"

"And I am going to bring her home," Wolfram said firmly.

"What if she is –?"

"Dead?" Wolfram said. "My brother wouldn't dare harm Alyssa," he added. "His bad blood is with me, not her; Alyssa is merely his pawn, she will be quite safe in his care."

"And do you know where they are? The forest is vast."

"I do not," Wolfram was honest, but not phased by the revelation. "But I have at least a good idea of where to begin looking."

With that, Wolfram strode purposefully from the room. "Have the stable boy get my horse ready," he ordered without so much as a backwards glance at the Mistress. "Unless you've tired him out too much, of course," Wolfram said with a deep, booming laugh that resonated along the stone hallway.

The Mistress allowed herself a wry smile at Wolfram's comment, the heated throbbing in her vagina a pleasant reminder of her earlier dalliance with the sweet young man amongst the straw and the overpowering smell of horses.

*

"Brecht is leaving to find the girl," Timur told the others.

"Then this is the opportunity we have been waiting for," Valentin said as he shuffled about on the edge of the orgy bed.

Bogdan climbed down from the bed and began pacing around its periphery; hands clasped behind his back much like the stance of an expectant father.

"We can make our move when he is out in the forest, whilst he is still weak from his brother's attack."

"We must make sure that he never returns," Pyotr's voice had a sinister ring to it, his blood lust already aroused.

Maxim said nothing, he was too busy eating. Yakou looked on in his customary silence as his co-conspirator ripped at the raw, bloodied flesh of the short haired girl's calf muscle, her slack body jiggling with each chunk of meat that Maxim tore away.

The bed was an absolute mess, and would take a considerable amount of cleaning up – Timor was pleased that there were at least a couple of servants who would take care of the blood, ragged shreds of flesh and spilled entrails without complaint; with Wolfram being incapacitated and the Six more or less in charge, the staff daren't do anything but comply in silence with whatever was asked of them. The three young women would be easy enough to replace. Once their bodies were disposed of, Bogdan and Valentin would be dispatched to one of the neighboring villages to recruit a handful more. There seemed to be an endless supply of nubile, willing girls who were so easy to seduce with promises of a fat wage and the opportunity to work at the Wolfram mansion. It was almost *too* easy at times, and no one in their villages appeared to question the whereabouts of the young maidens who simply disappeared.

"He is leaving soon," Timor said, licking the clotted blood from between his fingers. "We shall follow him into the forest and await our chance.

The other five nodded solemnly. Not one of them particularly relished venturing into the forest, even in their beast forms, yet to a man they knew that they had no other option. This was their one chance; their time was near.

As if on silent command, all six of the young men began their transformation, their naked, blood spattered bodies twisting and morphing in unison.

*

Alyssa had grown to love the forest.

In her werewolf state, even the darkest of the shadows that skulked between the trees held little fear; although having seen what a bear was capable of even with a seasoned werewolf like Sal, she always maintained a respectful wariness. Alyssa loved that she could now transform at will – full moon or not, day or night – and each transformation brought along with it the most sumptuous of orgasms; quite often she would cum hard and loud before Sal had so much as laid a hand – or *paw* – on her quivering, alight body. She loved that she and Sal would choose to live as beasts for days at a time; she enjoyed her animal self, and the sense of freedom that going completely feral brought with it.

And as for Sal, with each passing day spent naked in the cabin and amongst the majestic trees with him, she craved his huge, powerfully built body more and more, lusted after him like a bitch on heat, lived for the moments that he was deep inside of her, or lapping at her juicy pussy like it was the sweetest of sweetmeats. And so it came as no surprise to Alyssa to discover that she loved him.

Of course Alyssa was familiar with the concept of Stockholm syndrome, in which a captive develops feelings for their captor, but somehow her feelings for Sal felt like nothing quite so simple.

Sure, he had snatched her away from under Wolfram's nose, whisked her away to some remote corner of this foreboding forest where her only other human contact was the ever-delicious Darya and her eagerly accommodating pussy and tongue. And Sal had kept her captive in this place – her gaolers the densely packed trees who stood in silent sentry over Sal's cabin – although of late Alyssa had come to think of the place more as *home*.

Alyssa had noted that there was something conspicuous by its absence over the previous weeks of her incarceration – since *he* had kidnapped her right from under Wolfram's nose; she had not had one single period.

Her belly had developed a slight yet distinct swell to its normally concave curve; her breasts had grown ever so slightly larger and more sensitive to the touch. At first, Alyssa had put her expanding middle down to the rich meat from the deer they hunted down – often she would gorge herself on the raw flesh whilst the animal lay twitching and bleeding amongst the leaf litter – but in the past day or so, the obvious had become impossible to ignore.

"I think I may be pregnant," Alyssa confided in Darya.

"It does happen when you fuck so much," Darya said with a smile. She cupped Alyssa's breasts in her hands, as if weighing them. "And with your kind, early gestation is rapid." She gave Alyssa's tits a squeeze, her eyes lighting up at the tiny white droplets that oozed from their swollen tips.

"Although I have never seen it happen quite so quickly as this." She leaned forward and licked away the milk from Alyssa's over-sensitive nipples.

"Could it be that I was this way when Sal brought me here?"

"It is always possible," Darya said, nuzzling the trembling twin mounds of Alyssa's breasts. "Do you not remember your last cycle?"

Alyssa let out a heavy sigh of pleasure as Darya clamped her soft, warm lips around her nipple and began to suckle; the sensation of the milky fluid being *drawn* from her tit created a delightful prickling feeling in her clitoris. "No," she breathed heavily, "but I just put that down to the stress of everything that happened to me – sometimes I skip a period when I'm stressed out."

"So you have no idea whose child you are carrying?" Darya's voice was muffled against the firm flesh of Alyssa's breast, her mouth filling with hot, sweet milk.

Alyssa buried a hand deep into Darya's hair, pulling the girl's face onto her tits, urging her to drink more from her body. "Honestly?" she sighed. "I really don't."

Darya slipped a pair of wriggling fingers up inside Alyssa's tight, wet pussy, expertly homing in on the firm swelling of her G-spot. She massaged it whilst at the same time rubbing the pad of her thumb firmly on Alyssa's clit, feeding her own arousal with the excitement of driving Alyssa towards orgasm whilst she suckled greedily upon her breasts like an infant at its mother's teat.

Chapter Ten

The next day, Alyssa awoke in the late afternoon. Her sleep pattern had been all shot to hell, what with her and Sal's nocturnal activities, so that even when she didn't spend the night cavorting through the forest with him, Alyssa would sleep soundly until quite late in the day; much to her own amusement, Alyssa was actually becoming nocturnal.

Darya had left Alyssa's bed to prepare food. On the side where Darya had slept next to Alyssa, the indent of her naked body was cold; she had clearly been up for a long time. Alyssa stretched out, enjoying the feel of the cool sheets against her bare skin, and the delicate scents of sex that she and Darya had left behind in the wake of their long night of passion. Alyssa's breasts felt full again – if anything, *fuller* than before Darya had sucked them dry whilst fingering her to a shuddering orgasm. Alyssa flung off the sheets and examined her belly, marvelling at the slight upwards curve of her smooth skin, her belly button a tad shallower than she remembered it to be. Absently, Alyssa stroked the mound, unable to stop herself from wondering just whose seed was growing in there; it was a worry that began to slowly gnaw at her.

"Time to get up!" Sal burst into Alyssa's bedroom, his shirtless torso glistening with a light sheen of sweat. He had on his thick gloves, a sure sign that he'd been chopping fire wood out back. He paused in the doorway, his eyes soaking up the sight of his lover's gloriously naked body.

"Excuse me!" Alyssa feigned annoyance, making no attempt to cover either her exposed tits or pussy. "Can't a lady get any privacy around here?" she laughed.

"No Ma'am." Sal smiled at her, the gold in his eyes twinkling as they danced the length and breadth of her toned, smooth body. "I have a surprise for you," he teased. "Get dressed and join me outside – unless you'd rather remain naked to meet our guests?" A wicked glint shone in Sal's eye.

"Give me five," Alyssa told him, inwardly debating as to whether she should bother covering up or not – after all she did spend most of her time naked now, enjoying the sun's warmth on her skin and tired of ruining clothes whenever she transformed. And the fact that there were visitors held no worry for her, not after she had fornicated with Sal in front of an entire village! "I need to pee," she told him. "I'll be right out."

Sal left Alyssa to pee and get dressed, returning to the bright shafts of warming light outside, and the sun that was already beginning its late afternoon decline in the cloudless sky.

Alyssa clambered from her bed, attended to her ablutions and threw on her white dress, deciding against underwear – the waistbands of all of her panties were already beginning to feel tight.

Blinking against the harsh light beyond the cabin door, Alyssa was greeted by the sight of two incredibly attractive people. On the neat patch of grass at the front of Sal's cabin stood a man and a woman - obviously a couple – both of whom were at least six-one, six-two. They were dressed in Lycra – he topless in navy blue cycling shorts, she in clinging black booty shorts and a tight sports top that showed off her incredibly toned abs to perfection. As with his partner, the man's sharply defined musculature simply screamed long, arduous hours at the gym, each individual muscle bulging and taut against his perfect skin. Both were noticeably barefoot, their immaculately pedicured toes sinking into the rich green of Sal's grass.

"This is Maaria and Eadric," Sal made the introductions. "They don't speak much English."

"Hi," Alyssa greeted the pair and offered her hand to shake.

"Hello," Maaria replied, taking Alyssa's hand first and squeezing it in a grip so powerful that it made the tiny bones hand roll over one another. Alyssa looked up at the Amazonian woman, mesmerized by her dark blue eyes, set in an incredibly beautiful face that was topped with the blackest hair that was cut into short spikes that stood up from her head like tiny antennae. Next, Alyssa shook Eadric's hand – a similarly commanding grip and hearty shake. In contrast to Maaria, Eadric had richly hazel eyes and a smooth shaven dome of a head that shone brightly in the low sunlight.

"We have a little fun arranged," Sal explained, "I hope you don't mind."

Alyssa shook her head. No, she didn't mind. It certainly wouldn't be the first time she and Sal had invited others into their bed, although Eadric would be the first guy to join them. Alyssa felt a twinge within her vagina and she couldn't help but glance downwards at the impressive bulge in Eadric's shorts – the very thought of having that monster tucked between her thighs was making her wet.

"Shall we begin?" Sal said, somewhat formally. On cue, Maaria and Eadric peeled off their tight clothing and in the blink of an eye were entirely naked in front of Alyssa and Sal.

Alyssa didn't try to hide the fact that she was staring at the smooth shaven bodies of the couple. Not one single, solitary body hair marred their perfectly sculpted forms – from armpits to pudenda and beyond, every square inch of tanned, epilated skin was unabashedly on show. Alyssa was pleased to see that she had been right about Eadric's cock – even as flaccid as it was at that moment, it was gigantic and snaked down the side of his leg like some thick, third limb. As if not to be outdone, Maaria's pussy lips bulged out between the taut V of her toned thighs, its slit perfectly uniform, the slight bump of her clitoris head peeping out from the very top – it was, Alyssa thought to herself, an absolutely perfect *porn star* pussy. Maaria seemed to enjoy Alyssa's attention, shifting her legs ever so slightly apart and thrusting out her firm, gravity-defying breasts in order to present herself for the best scrutiny.

Alyssa began to pull her dress up over her head, more than keen to get this thing started, promising herself that she would spend more than a little time with Maaria's stunning body before sinking herself down onto Eadric's fat cock.

Sal placed a hand on Alyssa's arm, preventing her from undressing. "No," he said, his voice firm. "That is not what we are here for."

An awkward silence passed between the four, Alyssa doing her best to hide her disappointment from the gloriously naked couple who stood mere inches away from her wanton body.

"Are you ready?" Sal asked Maaria and Eadric.

Silently and in unison, they nodded.

Then they turned and ran.

Puzzled, Alyssa watched the magnificently toned buttocks of the naked pair as Maaria and Eadric ran full pelt towards the forest, their bare feet pounding hard on the grass to propel them forward at a pace Alyssa hadn't witnessed before in human beings.

"Now the fun starts," Sal said with a grin. He slipped his pants off, kicked off his shoes and began to transform, the familiar coating of dark, coarse hair sprouting across his broad torso as his face elongated and his long bones shuffled around in his legs.

So this was the game, Alyssa thought to herself as she watched the striking forms of the naked couple plunge into the murky gloom of the dense forest, reminding her of the show on TV that Rusty loved to watch – the one where they stuck two nude strangers in the middle of nowhere to survive for three weeks and blurred out their genitals. This was a *hunt*, pure and simple; Sal had brought the sexy couple here to offer a more cunning prey than the deer and boars that were plentiful in the mountainous countryside around the cabin. Alyssa wasn't too sure about how she felt about hunting down *people*, even in her werewolf form, the concept was entirely alien to her. Even so, she pulled off her dress and stood there naked, watching Maaria and Eadric as their honey brown skin vanished into the forest, their nude, vulnerable bodies swallowed whole by the dark, sinister undergrowth.

And then Alyssa began to change, embracing the myriad sensual pleasures that raced through her metamorphosing body as she became her animal self.

*

He didn't have to venture too far into the forest, for within a few hours of trekking through the thick undergrowth, Wolfram had caught the scent he'd been looking for; it was always so much easier to detect others of his kind once they transformed. And there it was, faint but distinct and wafting down from the side of the snow-capped mountain on the cool, gentle breeze.

His brother and Alyssa.

Both in their werewolf forms, soaked through with adrenaline from the thrill of the hunt, their animal fragrances mingling with the sharp tang of the pines.

Wolfram urged his horse northwards, homing in on his quarry, his keen nose also informing him that Alyssa was pregnant.

Wolfram had detected the weak odors of those who were following him; their scent nowhere near as distinct as they had chosen to remain in their human form – most likely for that very reason – but Wolfram knew that the Six were not too far behind him, and he had a good idea of their purpose. Nonetheless, he continued on his way, all the while working through in his sharp mind just what the best course of action would be – on both counts.

Ducking down to avoid a low hanging branch, Wolfram gave his horse a gentle dig in the flanks from his feet, coaxing the animal on as it pushed on through the darkening forest with a growing reluctance; it too could smell the werewolves and had to fight against its every instinct to flee in order to obey its master.

*

The light was dimming fast, and Timur had suggested they make camp and hunker down for the night; they knew now which direction Wolfram was heading and all they had to do was bide their time and await their chance to pounce. He selected a small clearing, opened up by the crashing demise of a massive tree during the previous winter's storms. There was a stream nearby, a crystal clear cascade of pure mountain water which was teaming with fat, wary fish.

"We should have brought a girl," Bogdan grumbled.

"We should have brought two," Valentin added, laying out his sleeping mat on the mossy ground.

"We cannot afford *any* distractions," Timur said. "I am sure you can do without village girls to fuck for a few nights."

Maxim huffed at this, his libido pretty much out of control for most of the time. "At least we would have had something to eat afterwards - instead of dammed fish."

"Who said we would be eating fish?" Timor said with a grin. He pulled out from his saddle bag a bulging, foil-wrapped package. He laid it on the ground next to the crackling heat of the fire Yakou had constructed and unwrapped it.

To a man, the Six salivated as Timur exposed the raw, bloodied flesh that nestled within the package.

"You saved some," Bogdan said. He dipped a hand into the flesh and pulled out a long sliver of calf muscle – it still had a strip of smooth, pale skin attached to it and that made his mouth water all the more.

"Should we cook it?" Maxim asked as he selected several delicately manicured fingers from the heap of oozing flesh.

"That's entirely up to you," Timur told him, "I much prefer to take my dinner raw." And so saying, he thrust a chunk of meat against his lips and bit off a succulent mouthful.

The others fell upon the girl meat like a ravenous pack of dogs, tearing through the flesh with fingers and teeth, their werewolf forms shimmering just beneath the surface of their human façade. They took great care to control it, though, sure in the knowledge that should they transform, Wolfram would detect their presence in the forest and so easily turn the tables.

It was, however, a precaution that came too late.

Once they had finished up the flesh - Pyotr and Yakou arguing over who was to get to lick clean the foil - Maxim declared that he was going down to the stream to wash himself clean by the light of the half moon that hung fat and bloated in the night sky above them.

Of course, the others knew *precisely* why Maxim was going to the stream, and half-expected him to invite one or more of them along. Much to everyone's surprise, he did not, preferring to make his way down to the cool, rippling water all alone. He had sated one appetite; it was time to deal with another.

Maxim stripped at the water's edge and stepped naked into the chill water of the stream. The silvery beams of the moon dappled his exposed skin, dancing their cold light over his firm, toned body. His stiff cock stood out and proud from his crotch, its thick, bulbous head pointed upwards, blue-veined shaft magnificent in the moonlight. Maxim wrapped a hand around his cock, his fingers gripping the shaft firmly and his thumb massaging the slippery dribble of pre-cum over the rubbery surface of the swollen head.

He stepped further into the stream, his legs disappearing into the water until his heavy, pendulous ball sack touched the coldness. This made Maxim gasp a little, the chilled ice-melt water caressing his balls, and although it had the effect of making them shrink towards his body, it heightened the pleasure that radiated out from his cock as he slowly but firmly stroked it.

Maxim stood there in the gentle current of the stream, his broad back to the darkness of the forest, the muscles in his torso tense and bulging as he worked diligently at his cock, all the while fighting the urge to transform into his werewolf state and enjoy the impending orgasm even more. But no,

Timur had been quite adamant about that particular point; they were all to resist the temptation to change until they had Wolfram cornered. The element of surprise was what would give them the edge against their nemesis; although Brecht Wolfram was older and still recovering from his injuries, they knew to a man that it would behove them not to underestimate him.

His strokes quickened, climax was fast approaching. Maxim cupped his cold balls with one hand whilst he worked his shaft and the bulbous, sensitive head of his long, sturdy cock. He held his breath and closed his eyes as the pressure built up inside his body, spreading out from his prostate to clench his balls even tighter to his body and create a hot tingle in the core of his dick. Then Maxim grunted as he climaxed, his raw, animalistic sound scaring away something in the undergrowth behind him. His hackles rose at the sound of rustling leaves and snapping twigs but his body was overridden by the wave upon wave of orgasm that tore through his senses.

As he came, Maxim's hips bucked involuntarily, fucking the cool air as thick, creamy white strings of ejaculate shot out from the eye of his cock to rain down onto the surface of the stream where it was carried quickly away by the rippling current. Maxim grunted again, unable to help himself as his balls emptied out, his hand still working on his thick length, determined to milk every last drop of cum – and pleasure – from his onanistic act.

He wasn't aware that he was not alone until it was much too late.

A great and powerful weight struck Maxim in the middle of his exposed back, toppling him forwards into the icy water with his cock still clutched firmly in one hand. The weight held him beneath the surface, the icy water invading his nostrils and mouth as he attempted to scream. He struggled, kicked and lashed out with flailing arms at the thing that had him pinned face down, his body mashed against the smooth pebbles on the stream's bed, his erect cock digging down between them.

Frantic, his life leaving him on the silvery bubbles of air that were forced from his lungs, Maxim began to change, desperate for the strength of his werewolf self to save his skin. Frantically, he willed his bones to begin their work of shifting about his body,

Alas, it was too little, too late. Maxim felt the pressure of huge jaws clamp around the back of his neck, the brutal stab of razor sharp teeth prickling his nape. And just as his face began to stretch outwards and the fur sprouted across his shivering body, the jaws snapped shut.

Wolfram pulled his head out of the water and watched the dark eddies of Maxim's blood as it swirled away downstream. The young man's limp body was stuck mid-transformation, like the perverse embryo of some hideous, impossible creature. He took his huge paw off Maxim's back, and the twisted corpse bobbed to the surface, blood pouring from the huge, ragged hole in his neck, the white nubs of exposed vertebrae glinting in the dim light. Wolfram turned the body over and upon recognizing Maxim's face he felt a slight pang of regret; he never liked taking the life of one of his own, even if he did know what fate Maxim and his group had planned for him. Boardroom business was one thing, but out here in the wild, only Mother Nature's rules applied – and those dictated *kill or be killed.*

Wolfram returned to the forest, barely making a sound as he crept through the scrub back to his horse, his body returning to its human form. He cast a quick glance backwards and saw Maxim's naked body floating face up in the stream, lazily making its way down the mountain, its cock still turgid and pointing angrily at the night sky like the mast of some sad, perverse boat.

Chapter Eleven

Maaria and Eadric had proved themselves to be formidable adversaries. They had managed to evade their werewolf pursuers for many hours, until the early darkness of night had descended like an ominous shroud upon the forest. But now, Sal and Alyssa were closing in on them, the stink of the young couples' fear-sweat was strong and an incredibly powerful aphrodisiac to the werewolves.

Alyssa kept close behind Sal, relying on his expertise to guide her through the thickest parts of the forest, densely packed trees and seemingly impenetrable thickets of hostile, thorny bushes that would have been impossible to traverse had they been in their human forms. Yet, somehow, the two naked people she had last seen outside Sal's cabin had made it this far; Alyssa could smell the faint traces of their blood on the bushes and the crispy leaf litter – the thorns had certainly taken their toll on those magnificent, nude bodies.

As she ran, Alyssa found that she was having some reservations about the hunt, about what the inevitable climax would bring. Despite her werewolf instincts having largely overpowered her human ones, she wasn't at all sure that she was ready to take that particular leap into the realm of the otherworldly creatures, although she knew that in reality this was her existence now.

Sal stopped, his body tense, the thick fur between his shoulders stiff and bristling. His long, thick tail swished gently side to side, his flanks heaving with heavy, controlled breaths as he sniffed the air ahead. Alyssa followed suit, her long, narrow snout lifted high, the black, shiny button of her nose dripping moisture onto the ground between her paws. She could smell them too, the piquant perfume of sweat mingled with the mouth-watering hint of fresh blood, of bodily fluids and adrenaline.

They had Maaria and Eadric cornered between a clump of young pine trees and a sheer rock face that scaled up impossibly high into the moonlit night. With Sal and Alyssa taking up the one and only escape route, there was simply nowhere for the sexy young couple to run.

Slowly, and with all of the stealth of a seasoned hunter, Sal crept forward with his belly low to the ground. Alyssa followed on, amazed with her own covertness and the fact that neither of then snapped so much as a twig as they advanced upon their prey.

Maaria and Eadric were bone-weary, their naked bodies grimy with dirt and emblazoned with myriad scratches from the unforgiving forest. They were pleased with their progress, at having kept at least a couple of steps ahead of their pursuers – right up until they came upon the sheet of granite that towered high above them. Here was no way to climb, for the rock was smooth and flawless as if honed by a master mason, and the trees were thick and too close together either side – even in broad daylight it would have been near on impossible for two exhausted, naked human beings to battle through. There was little more they could do now than sit with their aching backs against the coldness of the ancient volcanic rock and await their fate.

As things turned out, Maaria and Eadric didn't have all that long to wait.

They *heard* the werewolves before they saw them, as the moon's flimsy light was struggling to penetrate the overhead canopy of thick pine branches. What began as the subtle sounds of huge paws on the soft forest floor quickly gave way to the gently rustle of foliage parting around bulky, fur-clad bodies. And by the time the naked couple heard the deep breathing of the wolves, Alyssa and Sal were upon them.

Sal began to change the second he stepped out into full view of the couple who had led them so deeply into the forest. His fur receded, his bones snapped back into shape as he straightened his superlative body to once again walk on two legs. Alyssa followed suit, and soon the pair of them were as naked as their quarry.

As she followed Sal towards the Maaria and Eadric, studying the expression of resignation upon their gorgeous faces, Alyssa's doubts resurfaced, not helped in the least by the fact that she was once more fully human. She strode along nude, unabashed by her bare breasts and pussy in the presence of the two strangers, but a sick feeling in the pit of her belly.

"Must we do this?" she whispered to Sal as he stood over Maaria and her partner, touched by the way they held one another's hand so tightly. "We have had the fun of the hunt, couldn't we just -?"

Sal snorted and turned to face Alyssa. "What?" he growled.

"I said I don't think we should –"

Sal let out a laugh, his face crumpled with mirth. At his feet, and staring directly at his semi-erect cock, Maaria and Eadric joined in the laughter.

Alyssa stood there beside him, her body speckled with white shards of light, puzzled.

"What did you think we were going to do, Alyssa?" Sal chuckled.

"I thought –"

"You thought we were going to tear them apart and consume their flesh whilst they screamed and begged us for mercy?" Sal clearly thought this concept to be worthy of amusement. "What do you think we are? Animals?" He offered a hand to each of his supposed prey and helped them up from the ground.

Alyssa felt a mix of relief and disappointment, the latter of which surprised her. She offered a weak smile to Maaria, whose body was no less stunning for being covered in grime, scratches and smears of drying blood. Maaria smiled back, her hand still clasped in Eadric's, her eyes darting across Alyssa's naked breasts.

Still smiling, Maaria let go of Eadric's hand and approached Alyssa. And without hesitation, she took Alyssa in her powerful arms and pressed her hot, nude body into hers. She kissed Alyssa, her tongue snaking between her lips, the taste of her mouth hot and metallic. Alyssa greeted Maaria's tongue with her own, her hands groping at the young woman's high, firm breasts, fingers tweaking the taut nipples that sat atop them.

And then Eadric was behind her, his broad, buff body pressed into Alyssa's back, his cock hard and urgent, digging into the soft flesh of her buttock. Sal wrapped his long, strong arms around Maaria, his hands reaching all the way around to Alyssa, his hips squirming against his prey's taut butt as he manoeuvered his dick into the cleft of her ass, seeking out the warm slickness of her pussy.

"*This* is our reward," Sal said to Alyssa as he watched his mate slurp and suck and lick at Maaria's tongue. "It is also their reward for being such worthy opponents." And without the need for any further explanation, Alyssa knew just what was expected of her.

Maaria broke the passionate kiss with a wet slurp and lay herself down on the cool, mossy ground. She pulled Alyssa down with her and the two lay side by side, the bare skin of their hips and ribs pressed together. Maaria reached up to grasp Sal's hand, urging him down on top of her, guiding his broad, throbbing cock between her parted thighs. Eadric positioned himself over Alyssa, his eyes searching hers as if for permission.

By means of acquiescence, Alyssa grasped the young man's dick, amazed at just how hot and hard it felt between her fingers. She pulled it towards her supine body and spread her legs wide to give Eadric a full and uninhibited view of her wet, sweet spot. Needing no further encouragement, Eadric aimed his cock towards Alyssa and in a heartbeat he was sliding deep into the welcoming walls of her tight vagina, a serene expression upon his face as if hers was absolutely the best pussy he had ever experienced.

Lying beside Alyssa, Maaria let out a soft whimper as Sal buried his thick cock inside her aching, willing body – all the way down to its broad base until his heavy balls were squashed tight against the puckered brown rose of her ass. The thickness of Sal's cock – which Alyssa had grown so fond of – stretched Maaria's pussy and filled her sexy body as she bucked her shapely hips upwards to greet his, slamming her clit resolutely against the hardness of his pubic bone.

Sal and Eadric fucked Maaria and Alyssa in perfect rhythm; their strong, muscular buttocks thrusting up and down in perfect synchronisation in the cool night air, the silence of the forest resounding with the lascivious sounds of sweat-slicked bodies slapping against one another, the soft, wet *squish* of sodden pussies crammed so very full with fat cock, and the moans and grunts of four building orgasms.

Maaria came first, her voice rising high pitched and loud into the darkness. She plunged her hands into Sal's hair and pulled his head towards her bare shoulder. And as she continued her climax, and Sal pumped his semen deep into her vagina, Sal sank his teeth into the soft flesh just below Maaria's clavicle. Maaria screamed again and a trickle of blood dribbled from the bite wound, looking black as pitch in the dim light of the moon.

Alyssa bit down on Eadric's arm upon feeling the first of the young man's ejaculatory spurts – it was so strong that she actually felt the hot cream splashing against the rubbery nub of her cervix – the taste and feel of the young man's blood in her mouth was everything she had imagined it to be; boiling hot, slippery, metallic.

Maaria and Eadric screamed out in orgasmic delight, their screams rapidly turning to howls as they lifted their elongating faces up to the moon, their heavily perspiring skin sprouting a thick mat of silken fur.

So this was their just reward, what they had been craving all along; the hunt had merely been a form of foreplay, the fucking a suitable climax to that. They had proven themselves to Sal and had been honored with his bestowing upon them the power and immortality of the werewolf.

Sal and Alyssa also transformed into their werewolf forms, still joined together by respective cock and vagina to the new recruits and then, in their new forms, they all began their fucking anew.

Chapter Twelve

Early dawn in the forest reeked with a fresh *newness*, a sickly-sweet pine odor that reminded Wolfram of hospital bathrooms. The dampness of the air, the delicate dusting of mist that hung around the tops of the tallest trees, the aroma of decaying pine needles all fought to conceal the scent of his prey, as if trying its hardest to throw him off course.

Nonetheless, the distinctive perfume of his brother persisted in Wolfram's nose, as human as it was. He knew from the subtle changes in the odors that he was no too far away from the man now, that Alyssa was still with him, and that they had spent much of the night in their werewolf forms. There was also the hint of something else; the smell of two new wolves had suddenly appeared in the air, scents that had definitely not been there the night before.

"You really ought to quit doing that, brother of mine," Wolfram grumbled to himself as he nudged his horse on through the trees, its heavy hooves crackling in the drying pine needles. "We have enough wolves to contend with as it is." Wolfram wrinkled his nose, the old anger he harbored towards Salamao bubbling once more to the surface like a stubborn, pustulent wound; the hurt he felt still fresh and raw.

Then Wolfram's mind dashed back to the previous night, to the satisfying snapping of bones and rending of flesh that had signalled the demise of Maxim, and he wondered what the remaining five of the Six would make of the young man's sudden disappearance.

It wasn't long before Wolfram came upon Sal's home. This was the first time he'd seen where his brother had retreated to following that fateful night with Anichka what seemed to be a lifetime ago. It was modest - most likely built using his brother's own blood, sweat and muscle – a far cry from the majestic opulence of the Wolfram mansion, yet somehow it felt more like a home.

Staying within the seclusion of the tree line, Wolfram observed the house with keen vision. His nose informed him that his brother and Alyssa were not there, although they were not all that far away, yet there were signs of life within.

Shortly, the front door opened and the slight frame of a young woman stepped out. Clad only in tiny, white cotton panties, the girl breathed in the dawn air with a deep inhalation and she stretched her arms high above her head as she shrugged off he night's sleep. She smelled fresh and clean, her long cascade of silky black hair carried upon in a hint of soap and jasmine, her tiny body with its pert breasts and taut, dark pink nipples smelled unmistakably and entirely *human*. This intrigued Wolfram; why had his brother not turned the girl? Could it be that he had learned his lesson after all?

Wolfram watched the young girl awhile, with a familiar stirring in his loins. Her naked body fair shimmered in the sunlight, her hair iridescent. Her delicate, bare toes caressed the soft grass as she selected a handful of vibrant flowers from the lovingly tended flowerbeds that bordered the small lawn. And then Wolfram watched as she returned to the cabin, her peachy ass swaying provocatively, her ink black, flowing hair flowing like liquid about her unblemished shoulders.

With a mild kick of his heels to the horse's flanks, Wolfram turned back into the forest and followed the scent of his brother.

*

"I knew Max would show his true colors sooner rather than later." There was venom in Valentin's voice.

"We don't know that he has run away," Pyotr threw in. "He may be lost – we should at least try looking for him."

"He is a coward," Timur said as he urged his horse on through the forest. "We will deal with him upon our return, should he dare show his face again, that is." He snorted his derision and fell silent, a dark, brooding expression upon his handsome face.

Bogdan, at the head of the column signalled that they should stop. He halted his horse and sniffed the air. He then cocked his head – dog-like – as if the rattles and rustlings of the branches high above were talking to him. He raised an arm and pointed to some indeterminate point ahead of his horse's nose. He had no need to tell the others to be silent, that much was a given.

Darya was in the kitchen when the first of the horses emerged from the forest. It was rare that they ever saw people this deep in the forest, and rarer still that anyone came along uninvited. There was something about the five handsome young men on horseback that unnerved Darya and made her wish that Sal was home, something about the darkness of their gold speckled eyes that gave her a gnawing knot of unease in the bottom of her belly.

Quickly, she dashed to her room and threw a dress over her near-nude body, as much as she enjoyed the feeling of freedom that being naked afforded her, she had no desire to face five strange young men wearing nothing but thin, white panties that displayed the bulge of her pudenda and the slit of her sex.

"Anyone home?" Bogdan called across to the cabin. "Hello?"

"What is this place?" Valentin asked.

"Your guess is as good as mine," Timur replied. "But *he* has passed this way." He sniffed at the air as if to emphasize his point.

The door opened and Darya stepped out. Cradled in the crook of her arm was a long, twin barrelled shotgun. "Can I help you?" She said, doing her best to hide the tremble in her voice.

"Quite possibly," Pyotr replied as he dismounted.

The other four followed suit, leaving their horses behind them to approach the slight young girl with the pert breasts and the long, shimmering hair.

"We are looking for a man – somewhat older than us – who we believe came this way less than an hour ago." Timur said. He held his arms to his sides in a gesture of trust. "Did you see him?"

"No one has been by at all," Darya told him. "And I was up before dawn, so I would have seen anyone who passed by." Her fingers clutched the cold yet comforting steel of the gun.

"Are you sure about that?" Bogdan growled, his patience wearing thin, his libido rising in the presence of the sweet-smelling young woman. With hungry eyes he scanned her small, perfect body, paying particular attention to the way in which the hardness of her dark nipples pressed out against the soft white cotton of her dress.

"Quite sure," Darya stood her ground, her unease in the presence of the young men growing.

It was Yakou who stepped forward, as usual choosing to remain silent. He stood almost toe to bare toe with the girl, his dark brown eyes burning into hers.

"No one was here," Darya reiterated, desperate to take a step back from the imposing figure crowding her personal space, yet knowing that to do so would be to show weakness. "Now unless there is something else I can help you with, the master of the house will be home shortly –"

The five fell upon Darya, tearing the gun from her hands before she even had the time to fire off one round. She screamed and fought valiantly against them but their onslaught was too ferocious, too relentless for her small frame to have any effect. It was Valentin who tore out Darya's throat and a tall, bright arc of crimson shot up into the glimmering morning sunlight, falling upon the fur-covered bodies of the wolves who feasted upon

Darya's struggling body as she writhed in her final death throes.

*

Sal stirred, his naked body entwined with Alyssa's. Beside them lay Maaria and Eadric, still sound asleep; the nocturnal rigors of their new state of being would take them some time to adjust to. They slept the deep, heavy sleep of exhaustion, the exertions and thrill of the hunt followed by a full night's exploration of their werewolf alter egos had certainly taken its toll.

Alyssa awakened as Sal attempted to extricate himself from between her legs; she had wrapped them around his in the night and had made quite a knot of the pair of them. "I'm sorry, you go back to sleep," he whispered, but Alyssa was already wide awake by then; something had prickled her preternaturally keen senses.

Sal had sensed it too. There was something in the air that troubled him, a presence that he had detected as little more than subtle hints over the past few days, something he had dismissed as nothing more than a minor change in the wind. This morning, however, it had roused him from his dreamless sleep, prickling his animal senses that were never too far beneath the surface.

He stood up and brushed the dead leaves from his skin, enjoying the caress of the soft ground beneath his bare feet. He looked down at Alyssa with her full breasts and ever-rounder belly, marvelling at just how quickly her pregnancy was beginning to show. And then over at Maaria and Eadric, his new recruits to the werewolf species, their wish finally granted. He had enjoyed hunting them, their cunning and instinct for survival had impressed him, as had their sexual prowess; they had fucked for most of the night, in one of their forms or the other.

Alyssa struggled to her feet beside Sal, shivering slightly as the cool morning air caressed her naked skin. Her nipples stood immediately to attention and the chill draught on her bare clit sent a delicious twinge deep into her well-fucked pussy. "What is it?" she asked, looking up into Sal's deep, dark eyes.

"I don't know," Sal was honest with her. "But I think we ought to head back home now."

"We should wake them," Alyssa poked at Maaria with her bare toe, delighting at how the young woman's breasts jiggled; she would have given anything right then to be sucking on those soft, wide nipples and finger fucking that juicy wet hole whilst Eadric slid his fat cock up inside her own tender pussy.

"Let them sleep a little while longer," Sal told her. "At least until we finish dressing." He left Alyssa's side to collect his clothes from the forest floor where they had lain since the night before; although now they were damp and had tiny insects scurrying about on them. Alyssa did likewise, wrinkling her nose at the dank smell her dress had adopted overnight, promising herself that the first thing she would do upon returning to Sal's cabin would be to shower and spend the rest of the day naked.

Sal was pulling on his pants when suddenly he froze. He stood there, one leg in, one leg still bare, his cock dangling limp yet vibrant against his inner thigh. He stared off into the forest, his head tilted ever so slightly to one side. Alyssa made her way over to him, her moist dress sticking to her skin. "What is it?" she whispered. Sal silenced her with an uplifted finger, all of his attention focussed upon a black patch of the forest in which Alyssa could see nothing.

"Hello, brother," a voice said from behind them.

Sal jumped, turning around so quickly that he almost toppled over. Alyssa let out a cry and twisted her head in the direction of the disembodied voice, recognising it immediately.

"Brecht," Sal said as he faced his older brother. "I wondered when you would show yourself."

"Still falling for the old misdirection trick, I see." Wolfram's voice remained deadpan. He whistled and his horse made its way through the scrub towards them, from the direction in which Sal had been staring. "Hello, Alyssa." Wolfram's big, brown eyes looked her up and down, lingering upon the slight mound of her belly. He then looked across at Maaria and Eadric – still fast asleep – and sniffed at the air; the sharp stink of sex hung over them like a shroud, so much so that it was all but palpable.

"Hi," Alyssa said, her tongue sticking to the suddenly dry roof of her mouth. "I thought that you were –"

"– dead?" Wolfram scoffed. "It would take more than my little brother to put me in the ground," he added. "Are you okay?"

"I am," Alyssa replied, not at all sure what the right thing to say was, given the circumstances. "Salamao has done nothing to hurt me."

"Except to kidnap you and bring you to this god-forsaken end of the forest." Wolfram growled, his anger directed towards Sal. "What were you thinking, brother of mine?"

"I was thinking that it was time that I took from you what you took from me," Sal retorted, finally finding the wherewithal to pull his pants up over both legs.

"So this *was* about Anichka?" Wolfram stepped towards Sal. "I thought as much."

"I loved her, and you took her away from me." There was a tinge of sadness in Sal's voice. "Along with my child."

"You did not know for certain that the child she was carrying was yours, brother," Wolfram said. "She loved us both, and was equally free with her body – you know that."

"Then we have arrived at the same place, so many years on." Sal glanced across at where Alyssa's dirt stained dress clung damply to her stomach. "This child could belong to either of us."

Wolfram looked into Alyssa's eyes, as if searching for the innocence that he had seen in there all that time ago in the clinic and on their first and only night joined together. Of course, by biting Alyssa and indoctrinating her into the werewolf species he had been personally responsible for eroding much of that innocence. She was a werewolf now, an otherworldly creature of the night; a state of being that brought along with it its own voracious appetites and carnal desires.

"I'm sorry," Alyssa said, her voice quiet, barely a whisper.

"It is not your fault," Wolfram assured. "That lies entirely with my brother." He sighed. "And also with me, it was my selfish actions with Anichka so many years in the past that have caused this…this situation." He walked towards Alyssa and Sal, noting that his brother's body bristled, bones primed ready to shift and his canines lengthening in their sockets.

"There will be no need for that, Salamao," Wolfram said. "The time for fighting each other is long gone, what really matters right now is that Alyssa is carrying a Wolfram. Unless –"

Alyssa shook her head; a little offended that Wolfram would dare suggest such a thing.

"The Families are after our empire and our blood," Wolfram informed his brother. "If we are divided, we will certainly fall."

"I have no interest in your business," Sal stood his ground, mistrust in his eyes. "I gave all of that up the night Anichka died." A tear shimmered in his eye, magnifying the flecks of gold in its iris.

"Then if not for yourself, for the honor of the Wolfram name," Wolfram said. "Surely that is still important to you?"

There was a long, heavy pause.

Sal stood, silent and motionless and staring at his brother's face, examining the fading scars that lined up along one side – scars that he had put there.

"They made their plans whilst I was incapacitated," Wolfram broke the silence. "And now they are coming for me. If they find out about Alyssa's condition, they will kill her too."

"How many?" Sal grunted. He placed a protective arm around Alyssa's shoulders, felt her shiver.

"Five. There were six, but I thinned the herd a little last night." He cracked a rare smile and a twinkle flashed in his eye. "They have been smart enough not to transform, so I'm not a hundred percent certain as to their exact whereabouts. Suffice to say, I am positive that they will find me soon enough." He raised an eyebrow. "They will find *us*."

And thus the uneasy truce between the estranged Wolframs was formed. There was no particular defining moment, any heartfelt tears and conciliatory hug, just a bond forged by the threat of a common enemy. Alyssa was firmly in the middle, the child in her womb a catalyst of the truce; itself the ultimate target for those desperate to steal the Wolfram empire.

Chapter Thirteen

Upon awakening, Maaria and Eadric were somewhat surprised to discover the older man and his horse in their midst. Unashamedly naked in his presence, confident with their superlative human form, they greeted Wolfram in their native tongue as one would someone at a genteel cocktail party.

"It is good to meet you both," Wolfram shook hands with the two, his eyes glued to Maaria's hard, perfectly proportioned body. She returned the gaze, a hungry look in her eyes. A dark, wanton look.

"We should go," Sal broke the moment. The antsy itch at the back of his mind had returned, it was an itch that was impossible to scratch. He didn't know exactly why, but he *had* to get back to the cabin. He set off walking, Alyssa in tow. The still naked Maaria and Eadric followed on, with Wolfram and his horse behind them – all in all, the five of them made quite the bizarre posse.

Neither Sal nor Wolfram attempted to make any small talk, both preferring the sanctity of silence;

idle chit chat not only would have given their position away to those who were looking for Wolfram, but just one wrong word could so easily break the armistice between brother and brother. And right now, they needed that bond to hold true.

*

"Was it wise to have done that?" Valentin asked, wiping the black haired girl's blood from his chin and licking it from his fingers. There were shreds of her torn skin and flesh still trapped beneath his nails; they would take an age to dig out.

"Was she one of our type?" Timur asked.

"No –"

"- then she was *prey*; that is the natural way of things." Timur mounted his horse. He gave little more than a passing glance down at the bloodied mess of Darya's ravaged body that lay oozing blood and fluids into the neatly trimmed grass. "We ate well; fresh meat is always the best."

The others mounted their horses too – Valentin included – and the five headed away from the cabin and back into the forest. Wolfram's scent was stronger now, wafting down from higher up on the mountain, carried down on the fresh morning air – and it was getting stronger.

*

Wolfram paused at the stream to let his horse drink from the cool water and rest up a little. The burbling water looked different in the bright light of the mid morning sun, and Wolfram's mind cast back to the night before when he'd watched

Maxim's lifeless body bobbing up and down in the current that swept it away. Sal stood next to his brother, Alyssa by his side.

"We will be there soon," Sal said as a matter of fact, still in no mind to make small talk with his estranged brother.

"We must remain vigilant," Wolfram replied. He scanned the banks of the stream, his keen, wary eyes searching for the slightest movement.

Maaria and Eadric filled their bellies with the cool, refreshing water, scooping it up from the rippling stream with cupped hands. Thirst sated, they washed each other's naked bodies off with the chilled water, gooseflesh prickling their skin from toes to scalp. Alyssa watched the two with envious eyes, unable to believe just how toned their bodies were – how *perfect*. And there was she, of average height and with a swelling belly; soon she would be simply fat and ungainly and she wondered if Sal would find her quite so desirable then. Her eyes wandered downwards to Eadric's cock, nowhere near erect but of impressive size nonetheless, and she allowed herself a little daydream about just how good it had felt the night before crammed deep inside her pussy.

Alyssa also contemplated Wolfram, remembering the night of passion they had shared together, and just how wonderful his thick, powerful cock had felt sliding in and out of her sopping wet vagina. She knew she would always be grateful for the gift he had bestowed upon her that night, and secretly hoped that the were-child she was carrying was his; Brecht Wolfram deserved at least that much out of their deal.

And then there was Sal. The big, broad, be-muscled younger brother who was only a step or two away from being totally feral. She'd hunted alongside him now and had seen with her own eyes just how brutally merciless he could be with the deer, boar and bear that were their staple sources of protein. And yet her heart ached for him, her body craved his, her pussy tingled whenever he was in close proximity - its memory of his massive dick stretching her tight entrance making her shin glow all over.

"We should go," Sal announced with a glance over at Eadric and Maaria who were stretched out on a flat, grey rock drying their magnificent bodies. In the glittering light of the bright sun, their tanned, hairless skin glowed and gleamed like burnished brass. Maaria absently toyed with her pussy, quite possibly not even aware that she was doing so, most definitely not caring who may be watching. She gently rubbed her index finger along the deep groove, pausing to flick at the slightly bulging head of her clitoris. Her breasts rose and fell with each of her quickening breaths, each nipple deliciously hard and pointing up at the blue, cloudless sky. She looked over with some disappointment at the others when Sal's voice broke her moment, taking her time in pulling her finger away from her slit – it came away slick and glistening wet.

Wolfram mounted his horse and set off back into the forest, Alyssa, Sal and the naked couple following on behind; Maaria's full, bountiful breasts jiggling and swaying as she made her way with confidence through the undergrowth, her partner's long cock bouncing playfully against his thigh.

It took them another three hours or so to reach Sal's cabin, by which time the sun was high up in the sky and beating down upon Alyssa and the others with a relentless heat. Alyssa was pleased to see the rear of the house when they emerged from the forest; her legs ached and her dress clung to every inch of her perspiring body, its material soaked through with sweat. Wolfram – ever the gentleman – had offered her a place on his horse, but she had told him thank you, no. She had no desire to stoke the embers of resentment that still smouldered between the two brothers.

Sal manoeuvered himself to the front of the group. He grabbed hold of Wolfram's horse's bridle to bring the creature to a sudden stop. "Something is wrong here," he whispered, sniffing the air. Wolfram dismounted. He too sniffed at the hot forest air, his keen sense of smell assaulted by the sharp, metallic tang of copper.

"Darya?" Sal called out. He broke away from the others and raced towards the cabin.

Of course there was no reply.

Alyssa chased after Sal, Wolfram and the others close behind. She stopped dead in her tracks at the sight that greeted her at the front of the house.

The mangled remains of the young housekeeper lay drying in the sun, its spilled blood dark and crispy on the flattened patch of grass. Darya's face was ripped to shreds and unrecognisable; were it not for the blood matted cascade of shiny black hair, the mutilated corpse could have belonged to anyone. As Sal collapsed to his knees in grief by Darya's side, a thick cloud of fat, black flies arose from her remains. They rose up into the air no more than a man's height and circled around their prize, the buzzing noise of their tiny wings almost deafening.

"You!" Sal turned to face his brother, his tear filled eyes filled with hate and accusation.

"I did not do this, Salamao," Wolfram visibly staggered back beneath his brother's hateful gaze, as if Sal had delivered a physical blow.

"You killed her," Sal struggled to his feet. "You *ate* her." He paced towards Wolfram, his long, broad fingers flexing as the long, curved claws began to form at their ends.

"This was not me," Wolfram attempted to placate. "The ones who are following me – Timur and his co-conspirators – this is their work."

Sal ignored his brother, his body transforming as he walked, the pain and hate in his eyes burning bright even as his face changed around them. Wolfram stood his ground, refusing to follow his brother's example; to do so would have been interpreted as an admission of guilt.

"Everything I have, you destroy," Sal growled, his voice less than human. "Ever since you took Anichka from me."

"You have to believe me, Salamao," Wolfram stared up at the huge, lupine shape of his brother as it towered above him. "This is what they want, to divide us."

"It is you who has divided us," Sal's coarse, growling voice resounded deep in his chest. "I was prepared to trust you for the good of our family name. But now – this." He cast a glance over at the wreck of Darya's body. The flies had alighted on her raw, seeping flesh once more to continue their crawling, feeding and fucking. Sal swatted at Wolfram with one mighty paw, knocking his brother clean off his feet. Wolfram flew sideways, crashing to the ground, winded.

Alyssa dashed forward. "No!" she cried out. "Don't do this, Sal!" She felt strong fingers wrap around her arm as Maaria grabbed her to hold her back. Alyssa tugged against the naked woman's grip but saw no malice in her eyes; Maaria was doing this was for Alyssa's own safety. And so she stood there and looked on helplessly as her lover stood menacingly and with murderous intent over the one who was quite possibly the father of her unborn child.

There came a loud crashing sound from the forest around them. Distracted, Sal spun around and saw five huge horses galloping towards him, each one coming from a different direction. Atop each horse sat a werewolf, gold flecked eyes blazing bright and fixed upon both he and his brother.

Timur led the attack. As tempting as it was to have simply watched as the Wolfram brothers tore each other limb from limb, his own blood lust and eventually won him over. Timur wanted to be the one to taste the freely flowing Wolfram blood and feel their bones snapping between his jaws.

"Get Alyssa inside!" Wolfram shouted out to Maaria. "Now!"

Maaria complied, ushering Alyssa into the cabin with haste. Eadric held his ground, his nude body already well on its way to his werewolf form.

Wolfram clambered to his feet, claws lengthening, teeth elongating in his stretching jaws, all fear of his brother's intentions dissipated; ancient feuds would have to wait.

Sal focussed upon Timur's horse, the first one to reach him. He lashed out with one long, solid arm and tore out the animal's throat in one brutal motion. The horse crashed to the floor, its twitching body sliding along the grass – it was already dead by the time its brief momentum came to a halt. Timur leapt from the animal as it fell and launched himself at Sal, and with deadly precision he landed squarely on the other werewolf's chest. The two toppled over and rolled around on the soft ground with foaming jaws snapping at each other's throats and vicious claws raking flanks and thighs.

Wolfram was already fully transformed by the time Pyotr and Valentin reached him, his razor-sharp claws at the ready. Behind him, Eadric was struggling with his change - still very much the novice – his body stuck somewhere between human and lycanthrope.

The two assassins jumped from their mounts before they reached their intended victim, choosing to attack Wolfram from the ground. They leapt at him in unison, a deafening, guttural yowl issuing from their lupine throats. Wolfram was ready for them. Although they had the advantage of youth, he had centuries of experience to counter that. The first swipe of his claws tore Valentin's face clean off of his skull, leaving nothing more than bloodied bone and naked, dripping teeth. Valentin howled in agony, his one remaining eye rolling wildly in its denuded socket as he clutched at his elongated snout with desperate hands. And even as Valentin crashed down to die in the dirt, Pyotr was upon Wolfram, his long, curved claws grasping for the older werewolf's throat.

Sal quickly learned that Timur's size was no indication of an inability to fight. The smaller werewolf seemed to be everywhere at once, ripping clumps out of his pelt with his scratting claws and digging lengthy ruts in his flesh with long, sharp teeth. Sal managed to twist his head and clamp his jaws around his assailant's forearm, taking great delight at the crackling noise the werewolf's twin bones made as they splintered between his teeth. Timur screamed loudly, the pain serving to fuel his frenzied attack, his snapping, snarling teeth tearing a jagged, bloody hole in Sal's ear.

Bogdan and Yakou headed towards the cabin, skilfully manoeuvring their horses around the melee and their fallen comrade, entirely ignoring the half man – half wolf who appeared to be quite bewildered by the changes his own body was attempting. They dismounted and rushed into the house, their mission clear; to neutralize the heir to the Wolfram empire.

Maaria was ready for them, her own transformation having gone far smoother than her partner's. She stood in front of the door, her werewolf body every bit as magnificent as her human form, and braced herself for the attack. Alyssa stood behind her, stripped naked and undergoing her own transformation, her body trembling with adrenaline and fear.

Bogdan crashed through the door with a piercing howl, the dark fur on his bulky body bristling. He ran directly towards Maaria, determined to go straight through her if necessary, eagerly anticipating ripping through the taut, firm flesh that rippled beneath the she-wolf's silken fur. Yakou ran in behind him, his sights set firmly upon the ultimate prize and not in the least bit phased by Alyssa's almost complete transformation into a deadly beast. He'd tackled bigger and stronger in his time and tearing the Wolfram child from her mangled womb would be a breeze.

Outside, Wolfram found himself to be pinned to the ground by Pyotr, the younger werewolf's youthful strength and larger size overpowering him. Wolfram's jaws snapped impotently in mid-air, his head restrained by the powerful paw that was deliberately crushing his throat. Desperately, he looked over at Sal, only to see that his brother was succumbing to the relentless onslaught of Timur, his face a mask of glistening wet crimson, his body torn and bloodied where clumps of his pelt had been ripped away. Wolfram's thoughts darted to Alyssa and a fraught feeling of helplessness swept through him; it was her child they were after, the first natural born werewolf in over two hundred years. Without the child, and with he and Sal dead, the empire would fall into the hands of the Families.

Suddenly Pyotr was gone. The weight of his body vanished from Wolfram in a heartbeat. There came the sound of a surprised yelp, followed by a dull thud of a huge body hitting the ground. Wolfram looked up, gulping down welcome breaths of warm air through his throbbing throat. He saw Eadric – still not entirely werewolf nor human – perched upon Pyotr, his half-human snout buried in the werewolf's chest. With an inhuman snarl and a violent shake of his head, Eadric tore out Pyotr's heart in one big, bloodied clump. Pyotr screamed out in pain and surprise and in the instant before life abandoned him, he actually saw his own beating heart.

Maaria and Bogdan fought in near-silence, their only sounds the panting of breath and scratting of claws on the polished wooden floor. At first they circled one another, swiping with ferocious claws, lunging with long, drooling fangs until finally they flew at each other with such animal brutality that the snapping of their ribs sounded out like a volley of gunshots. Maaria's superior strength and agility quickly outclassed Bogdan and before he knew what was happening, she had raked her rear paws the full length of his belly. He grunted and the fight drained from him, his teeth no longer snapping at Maaria's face. She stepped back from him, her body tense and ready to strike, puzzled at this sudden change.

Bogdan struggled to his feet, standing facing Maaria on all fours, his snout twisted in a grimace that almost resembled a cruel grin. There came a wet slopping sound, a splash of warm fluids as Bogdan's innards spilled from the ragged rent in his belly. He looked down, dumbfounded at the pink coils of intestines that cascaded from his ruined body, as if amazed at how they slid and slipped between his feet like long, glistening eels.

Maaria stepped away. The stink of the werewolf's guts forced the bile up in her throat and she fought hard to keep the nausea at bay – there was no time for such things, for her attention switched in the instant Bogdan lay down to die to Alyssa and the werewolf that had chased her to the rear of the cabin. A piercing howl split the air, spilling in through the broken door. Maaria looked out into the brightness beyond the splintered wood and saw Sal standing high on his hind legs, the entire upper part of his body drenched in blood. And in the splintered claws of one hand, he clutched the severed head of the werewolf who had launched the attack.

Wolfram came hurtling through the door, and hot on his heels came Eadric – Maaria was relieved to see that her partner appeared to be unharmed, if somewhat odd in appearance.

From upstairs there came the sounds of vicious snarling and the unmistakable thud of heavy furniture being overturned, wood crashing onto wood. At this cue, Maaria sprinted through the cabin and up to the first floor, Wolfram and Eadric close behind her.

Alyssa was standing her ground, Yakou trying his best to launch an attack against the angry, snarling beast she had become – he had her almost cornered, which was making her all the more aggressive. That, and her inherent mother's instinct; Yakou knew that she would protect her child until the very end, which was fine by him. He lunged again at Alyssa, this time his teeth making contact with her shoulder. He clamped on tight and chewed down on her flesh, eliciting a sharp squeal of pain. Alyssa shook and clawed at Yakou, sending tufts of his fair colored pelt flying in all directions, dismayed that her efforts were having little effect on the much bigger werewolf.

The bedroom door flew open.

Maaria, Wolfram and Eadric spilled into the room, canines bared, fur bristling, sharp, jagged claws click-clacking on the hard floor. Undeterred by the sudden intrusion, Yakou wrestled Alyssa to the floor, his teeth seeking the softness of her throat.

And then Maaria was upon him.

Yakou shrugged the she-wolf off like she was nothing more than a troublesome biting insect. Her body flew the full length of the room and crashed into the vanity mirror, shards of glass raining about her head. He clamped his jaws firmly around Alyssa's throat, feeling the pulse of her jugular against his tongue and that made him salivate; her blood was going to taste so very, very sweet. Alyssa kicked and struggled against him with all of her might, but Yakou was simply too big and too strong for her to gain anything from her fighting. She twisted her head side to side, gasping for air through her windpipe that was narrowed to a pinprick by Yakou's powerful bite, her vision clouding over with thick, black shadows.

Wolfram gathered every ounce of strength and knocking Eadric out of the way – in his half and half state he was more likely to get himself and Alyssa killed – he charged at Yakou's exposed back.

But Yakou was ready for him. He released his grip on Alyssa's throat, replacing his vicious teeth with one mighty paw and bit at Wolfram's face as the wolf bared down upon him. He felt part of Wolfram's upper lip tear away, caught the tangy flavor of fresh werewolf blood. Undeterred, Wolfram snarled and growled and kept up his attack, his frothing saliva running bright with scarlet, his curled claws seeking purchase in Yakou's thick fur.

Alyssa wriggled out from under Yakou's grip, his razor claws tracing deep red lines through the soft fur of her throat. She brought up her own claws and whilst Yakou was doing his damndest to tear away Wolfram's face, she ripped Yakou's balls clean from his body.

Yakou's throes of agony threw Wolfram off his body, sending the older werewolf crashing against the thick wooden posts of the bed, the sheer force splintering one of them amidst a rending cacophony of shattered wood and the shattering bones of

Wolfram's spine. All thoughts of Alyssa and her child were instantly forgotten as white hot sheets of agony shot through Yakou's body as he gripped at the bloodied hole where his testicles had once been. Blood pumped through his claws as he began to change back to human, Yakou's body no longer under his control, some parts returning to human, others remaining lupine.

Alyssa threw Yakou's balls onto the floor beside him, shreds of flesh hanging from her claws in thin, sickly strings. Oblivious to his howls of pain, she padded over to where Wolfram's still body lay and licked at his bloodied face. She looked up, across the room and saw Sal enter, his face as blood drenched as his brother's.

Sal said nothing.

He stalked across the room, studying Yakou's suffering as he walked by; the assailant was practically entirely human now and he now looked nothing more than sad and vulnerable. A thick pool of coagulating blood had spread out around his hips, his crotch and hands drenched and sticky with the stuff. He looked up at Sal as he stepped by, his eyes imploring for mercy.

Sal ignored him, in no mood for mercy nor delivering the *coup de grace;* Yakou was finished now whether he lived or died – his cohorts slaughtered and himself in no position to continue *his* family line. Sal sat by Alyssa's side and studied the lifeless form of his older brother, and all feelings of hate evaporated in that moment. He sighed sadly and rested a huge, bloodied paw on Alyssa's belly, sensing the new life that stirred within.

Chapter Fourteen

It was good to be back in the mansion again; Sal had missed the place. As sprawling and cold as the place was, it had been his home for many years and he had grown to love its every nook and cranny.

They had burned his cabin in the forest to destroy all traces of Timur and his traitorous gang – the families could spend eternity looking for them for all Sal cared; that would be a small price to pay for the death of his older brother. The pain of that loss still hung around Sal's neck like a leaden weight, the passing of half a year doing little to bring comfort.

But for now, he had the more earthly pleasures to distract him, the seemingly endless parade of willing young flesh to sate his carnal desires, and the deep love that he shared with his brother's would-be surrogate.

For her part, Alyssa had done everything she could to relieve her lover's pain and guilt, and hoped that her ever expanding belly would help keep his mind occupied. She was due sometime within the next few weeks, although the baby appeared to be more than keen to be free of its confines already, if the kicking and squirming was anything to go by. It didn't seem to matter to Sal whether or not the child was his – he had no desire to ever know, he'd told her – *it's a Wolfram, and that's all that matters.*

End of discussion.

They'd kept Maaria and Eadric around; they made for great staff, reassuring guards and incredibly imaginative sexual playmates. In her state of near constant arousal – quite common in pregnant she-wolves, the Mistress had informed her – Alyssa would spend many happy hours licking, sucking and fucking the pair of them, more often than not with Sal joining in to sate his carnal desires.

And then there were the orgies, organized on a scale the likes of which Wolfram Mansion had not seen in many centuries; comprising at times dozens upon dozens of incredibly wealthy and highly influential hedonists who would descend upon the place for week-long fuck-fests that involved every perversion Alyssa could ever have imagined, along with many that she could not.

This was to be her final orgy before the birth of her child, and Alyssa was determined to make the very most of it.

Everyone was entirely naked, not a shred of clothing as far as the eye could see, just an incredible expanse of naked human skin of every conceivable hue. Alyssa walked amongst the cavorting revellers, totally naked herself, her heavy, milk-engorged breasts swinging free over her massively swollen belly, her hairless pussy wet and glistening and ready to be fucked.

Alyssa paused by a small group of five party goers, three guys and two of the most stunning Asian girls Alyssa thought she had ever seen. She wriggled her body between the entwined group, grasping the long, hard cock of the one guy who appeared to be somewhat left out – his two companions were standing side by side in front of him, the two delightfully hot, naked Asian girls sucking noisily on their dicks. Alyssa knelt down in front of the third guy, her bare buttocks pressing against those of the two girls, delighting in the feel of their warm, smooth skin. She snuggled the guy's rock hard cock between the huge, twin mounds of her breasts and slowly began to massage it.

As she fucked the guy's cock with her cleavage, Alyssa kneaded the soft, pliant flesh of her tits, coaxing out dribbles of thick, creamy milk. The milk trickled down along Alyssa's cleavage and onto the purple, bulbous head of the guy's cock.

"Oh, fuck, that is so good," the guy moaned. He gripped Alyssa's bare shoulders and bucked his hips towards her, grinding his dick deep into the hot, wet, dark valley between her breasts.

"Are you going to cum on my tits?" Alyssa said, looking up into the man's eyes that were half-closed in ecstasy. "Shoot your creamy load over my hard nipples?"

That was all the guy needed to tip him over the edge. "Fuck!" he cried out, his voice rising above the subtle moans, groans, slurps and slapping of hot, sweating flesh in the ballroom. His hips jerked and bucked wildly as he lost all control and ejaculated between Alyssa's breasts, his cum shooting out from the bulging tip of his cock in thick, creamy white ropes.

Alyssa massaged the hot, salty cum into her tits, covering the entirety of her quivering mounds with slick, glistening juice. She rubbed it into the hard, jutting points of her nipples, teasing them to fully erect and sighing at the waves of pleasure that elicited through her nude body. She looked up into the guy's eyes as she did so, pleased to see the look of sheer pleasure – and gratitude – on his face, as she rubbed the tip of his twitching cock in small circles around her areolae, teasing herself with the hot, sticky, rubbery flesh.

And then she was done.

Alyssa stood up, her tits sticky and wet from the guy she had just pleasured, and stepped away from the group; he had the benefit of youth and remained hard, his cock far from spent – it would, no doubt, be buried to its hilt in some young pussy before too long. Alyssa looked down at the Asian girls and saw that as their heads bobbed up and down, mouth fucking their men, they were busy fingering each other, their long, nimble digits buried knuckle deep in one another's dripping wet vaginas. For a moment, Alyssa considered staying with the group, part of her longing to add her fingers to the two hot Asian pussies, entwining hers with the girl's until she made the two cum hard and loud and unbelievably wet on her hands.

But no, there were myriad pleasures to be had at the orgy, an almost endless variety of fornication through which Alyssa could derive her pleasures; she had certainly come a hell of a long way from that curious little virgin who'd first met Brett Wolfram in the clinic a lifetime ago.

Alyssa made her way over to a corner in which a particularly attractive couple were fully immersed in each other. The man was kneeling before his woman, his long mane of silken black hair draped all the way down his back. She stood with the wall for support, one leg lifted high on the window ledge to provide an unhindered access to her sopping, smooth pudendum. The man's face was pressed up against his lady's pussy as he lapped at her sex like he was drinking the finest of nectars, whilst his lover had her head thrown back and eyes closed tight in paroxysms of pleasure. Alyssa tapped the guy on his shoulder and he turned to face her, his face dripping wet from nose to chin with deliciously scented pussy juices. He smiled at Alyssa, recognising her immediately, and graciously he backed away from the swollen, pouting pussy he had been so diligently eating out.

Alyssa took the guy's place between the lady's legs and moved her face towards the mouth-watering dark pink flesh of her pussy; Alyssa inhaled deeply, her own vagina twinging with pleasure at the wonderful scent of the other woman, and she peered at the tight dark hole and the tiny, bulging head of the clit that poked out from beneath its hood.

Unable to contain herself any longer, Alyssa placed her mouth over the lady's pussy, running her tongue the full length of the sodden slit, flicking at the hard nub of the clitoris and drinking down the copious juices that fair poured through her lips. The lady sighed out loud and buried her hands in Alyssa's hair, welcoming the hot mouth of another onto her sex; gently she pressed Alyssa's face ever harder onto her crotch grinding her pussy into her face. Alyssa responded by sucking the woman's stiff clitoris into her mouth, drawing it in between her lips and rubbing its sensitive head with her tongue.

"Oh," the woman moaned out loud, "you horny bitch."

Alyssa smiled, delighted that she was creating so much pleasure in the woman. She reached up with one hand and began to explore the lady's tight, slick hole with her fingers, wriggling two up inside to stroke the hot, crinkled walls.

Behind Alyssa, the guy – clearly not wanting to be left out – was busy rubbing his cock on her ass. The hot, hard flesh slid between her shapely buttocks, made slippery with a generous application of the guy's saliva. Alyssa shuddered with delight as she felt the warm, wet juice trickle over her puckered hole, and she lifted up her ass the best she could to welcome the guy's bulbous cock head there.

Taking encouragement from this, the guy pressed his cock against the taut entrance and rocked his hips in time to Alyssa finger fucking and licking at his woman. At once, Alyssa's muscles relaxed and the guy's cock slid inside her ass with ease – all the way to its base in one easy motion.

Alyssa groaned as she was penetrated, pleased to have something inside her body. The soft vibrations of her voice made the woman moan loudly, her body dangerously close to climax.

It took all of Alyssa's resolve to pull away from the couple, the taste of the lady's pussy was so incredibly intoxicating, the feel of the man's broad girth filling her ass so wonderfully full difficult to give up. Yet, move she did, her face dripping wet with slick, piscine juices, her ass tingling from being stretched so. The couple wasted no time at all in reconnecting, and Alyssa helped guide the man's cock up into the pussy she had been eating out, taking great delight in feeling its hot, hard meat sliding inside the sodden flesh of the woman's vagina, slipping by her fingers like some eager, living thing.

Alyssa moved on as the couple fucked each other with rampant urgency, grunting and growling like caged animals, their damp, perspiring skin slapping noisily, the lady's perky breasts jiggling and bouncing with abandon.

Sal appeared by Alyssa's side, his magnificent, naked body glistening with a sheen of sweat, his huge cock rock hard and slippery wet with the pussy juice of one – or more – of the beautiful young hedonists. He took her hand and led her to the dead center of the ballroom. The sea of naked bodies parted to allow them through, until Sal and Alyssa took their place.

They kissed.

At first tender, but quickly turning urgent and forceful, Alyssa and Sal invaded one another's mouths with wet, thrusting tongues, tasting each other and the flavors of the others they had dallied with that evening. Sal then eased Alyssa to the floor, where she positioned herself on her hands and knees, her pregnant belly and heavy, leaking breasts hanging below her. She smiled at the crowd, those closest eyeing her fecund body with hungry looks, some salivating at the sight of the white milk that dripped onto the hardwood floor from her fat, swollen nipples.

Sal took his place behind Alyssa, his long, broad cock aiming at her upturned rump, its eye fixed firmly on the tight dark hole that winked from between her puffy labia. And then without further ado, Sal plunged his cock into Alyssa's pussy, its length gliding into her with slick ease.

"Oh," Alyssa moaned, her breath taken away by the sudden penetration. She felt her muscles clamp tight around her lover's cock, and her clit throbbed as Sal's thrusts pulled on its hood.

Sal began to change.

The strong hands that gripped Alyssa's hips as he fucked her sprouted long, curved claws as his body bristled with long, luxurious hair. There were gasps from the crowd as his torso widened and his legs took on their unmistakable lupine shape. And although Alyssa couldn't see from her position, Sal's face began its shifting and rearranging, its elongated snout gaping wide to show off the formidable array of curved, sharp teeth. And all the while, he thrust hard into Alyssa's pussy, driving hard towards his own orgasm.

The feel of her lover's transformation heightened Alyssa's pleasure a thousandfold. His cock expanded inside of her, its length and thick, bulbous root stretching her sensitive flesh to provide almost unbearable pleasure. She raised her butt even higher, and pushed back to meet Sal's thrusts, delighting in the incredible *stuffed full* feeling his werewolf cock gave her vagina. And as she countered her werewolf lover's hard, fucking strokes, Alyssa's bare breasts bounced and wobbled and leaked – there formed quite the wide puddle of milk beneath her.

As if Sal's transformation had been the cue they were waiting for, the naked participants of the orgy began their own metamorphosis. Fur sprouted, bones creaked, cracked and moved, teeth grew –

and all the while they licked and stroked and fucked. And as Alyssa watched, all around her the people changed into their werewolf forms that were equally as beautiful as their human appearance. And how they fucked – hard and fast with a furious, animalistic fervor – biting and snarling and howling as they worked at their pleasures, locked together in pairs, threesomes and moresomes in what had become an undulating sea of writhing, fur-covered bodies.

Alyssa held off her own transformation, relishing being the only human amongst the copulating crowd of ethereal beings, loving the feel of Sal's werewolf cock buried deep inside her still-human pussy. He drove it hard into her, the coarse fur of his belly rasping against the soft skin of her buttocks, making them tingle and ache to be spanked. It took all of her resolve to remain in her naked human form, her sexual senses racing ahead of her, every nerve ending in her body firing at once, the orgasm building up inside of her body like it was an unstoppable beast all by itself.

She finally succumbed to her werewolf self when she came. The climax ripped through Alyssa's body and she screamed and yowled, and as she let go, her body swiftly changed as Sal reached his own orgasm and came deep inside her werewolf pussy which in turn clamped down tight on the base of his cock, locking them together in an intimate embrace.

When it was over, and her pussy had released Sal's still tumescent cock, Alyssa and Sal had regained their human form and took their place to observe the ongoing orgy – the majority of their guests had no intention of giving up either their werewolf status nor their unbridled fucking.

Alyssa sat in Sal's lap whilst the King and Queen of some small African country suckled at her engorged breasts, gulping down her sweet milk like it was Nectar from the gods themselves. Alyssa caressed their soft, mahogany skin as they drank from her, lost in her own ecstasies as Eadric lapped at her clitoris with his ever so eager tongue, his fingers rhythmically fucking her soaked pussy hole. He paused momentarily to suck Alyssa's juice from his fingers, slipping them back inside her vagina to continue his work. Eadric had finally mastered the art of transformation and when he was in his full werewolf form, he became something that seemed to drive the female revellers into a soaked pussy, sexual frenzy. His partner Maaria, had decided upon adopting her wolf form for this particular occasion, and she was attracting the attention of a whole bunch of virile young men with eager, rock-hard cocks who were fighting amongst themselves to fuck the insanely hot she-wolf.

Alyssa sighed as her orgasm neared. She looked out across the sea of furry, writhing bodies that filled the mansion's ballroom, inhaled the heady scent of raw, unadulterated, animal sex and relished the feel of the naked skin against her fingertips. Her breasts throbbed and glowed at the attention of the pair who suckled at her fat, finger-thick nipples – Alyssa imagined that they were living, breathing things, entirely independent from the rest of her body, little more than corpulent milk creatures.

She could feel Sal's cock, hard and urgent deep inside her ass, its fat rubber head pulsing against the hot, crinkled walls of her insides. He would cum again soon, as would she, and his fluids would fill her body once more as she screamed out her climax.

And the feel of Sal's thick shaft stretching her sweet puckered hole took Alyssa's mind all the way back to Rusty.

Ahh yes, good ol' Rusty with his red beater truck and inherent, pious love of God's hole.

If only he could see her now.

The End

About the Author

 Jennifer Lynne is a lifelong advocator of all things hedonistic, and a writer who loves what she does - writing exactly the type of steamy erotica stories that get her personally hot under the collar.

In her objective to provide intelligent, wonderfully written and thoroughly engaging tales with something for everyone, Jennifer Lynne leaves no subject untouched and no taboos unbroken!

Every story is lovingly crafted with a beginning a middle and an end, with believable characters and an engaging plot that explores the most sensual, erotic and often sometimes darkest fantasies.

Jennifer comes from a varied career in the sensual pleasures, having organized hedonistic parties for the rich and famous, run an agency that catered to the bespoke fantasies of an exclusive clientele (some of which feature anonymously in her tales of debauched sex and lust) and toured her native England as the burlesque striptease performer Peachy Derriere.

Jennifer sincerely hopes that you absolutely love her stories - they are for ladies, for gentlemen, for couples to read together - and if there she always loves to hear from her fans; eroticjenniferlynne@gmail.com

There's something for every taste in Jennifer Lynne's extensive library of erotic short stories and collections at;

www.jenniferlynneerotica.com

Other Erotic HellBound Books For You To Enjoy

Available from www.hellboundbookspublishing.com

**Depraved Desires
(Coming April 2017)**

A mind-blowing collection of dark erotica from the very best minds in the business!

Feeder/I Am Joe's Unwanted Penis
By
James H Longmore

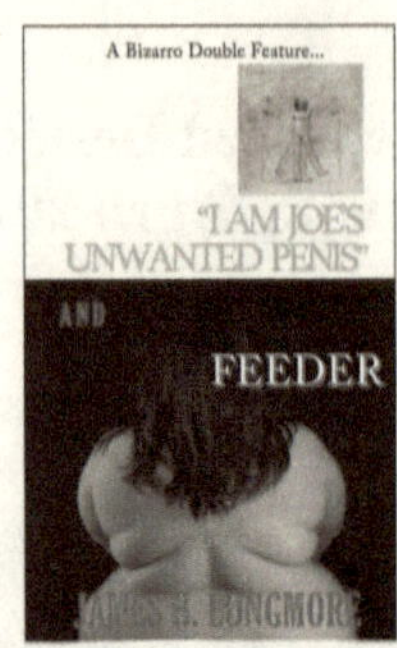

An awesome bizarro double bill...

'I am Joe's..." is an affectionate homage to the much-loved Reader's Digest series *'I am Joe's.'*, and a darkly humorous and bizarre parody of the Bruce Jenner story, this story is told from the point of view of a dismembered penis.

Feeder is a dark, disturbing peek into the world of gainers and feeders; grotesquely obese individuals and the people who facilitate their growth for the lascivious pleasure of both parties.

The Erotic Odyssey of Colton Forshay
By
James H Longmore

A stunningly imaginative bizarro tale in which Colton Forshay dreams himself into a bizarre sexual dystopia, a world in which nothing is as it should be. Sickening sex acts and sexual violence are the norm and in which the currency is deviant sexual acts.

At first disturbed, then intrigued - and aroused - by his dreams of this other world, Colton is drawn deeper in and begins to spend more and more time there; so much so that his wife forces him to visit a psychiatrist.

The psychiatrist encourages him to explore the dream world - and our hero goes on an odyssey with his dog/son, Eric, to discover the disturbing truth behind his dream world.